John George Hilzinger

The skystone - A Romance of Prehistoric Arizona,

Being vol. I of the Chronicles of Mázacl

John George Hilzinger

The skystone - A Romance of Prehistoric Arizona,
Being vol. I of the Chronicles of Mázacl

ISBN/EAN: 9783744641210

Printed in Europe, USA, Canada, Australia, Japan

Cover: Foto ©Andreas Hilbeck / pixelio.de

More available books at **www.hansebooks.com**

J. GEORGE HILZINGER.

THE SKYSTONE

A ROMANCE OF
PREHISTORIC ARIZONA

BY

J. Geo. Hilzinger

Being Vol. I of the Chronicles of Mázacl

F. TENNYSON NEELY

PUBLISHER

LONDON   NEW YORK

INTRODUCTION

THE introduction to a romance does not, usually, receive much attention from the reader, but an exception should be made in this case, for the reason that what is here written is necessary to a proper comprehension of what follows.

In the Salt River valley, in central Arizona, the ruins of at least seven large cities are conspicuous, and the lines of ancient irrigating canals can be traced over the level land for miles.

It has been assumed, with some reason, that the ancient inhabitants of the valley were akin to the pre-Aztec race that built the grand temples that yet rear their heads in Mexico and Central America.

They lived in *adobe* and cement houses, often several stories in height, and their main castles or temples were of grand size, defended by walls and towers and encircled by moats.

Their government was probably a theocracy, similar to that of the Hebrews after the exodus. They wove cloth, a few fragments of which have been preserved, were skillful in feather-work, utilized the skins of beasts, and made baskets and pottery with artistic skill.

They worked turquoise, shells, and certain spars into ornaments and images; and some of the latter, evidently portraits, are marvelous in their faithfulness to nature, showing not only the details of dress but the expression of countenance.

They understood the use of money, their principal currency being turquoise and shells worked into regular shapes, and usually perforated for convenience in carrying.

They had a written language, probably ideographic in part, though not entirely so, and their records were not carved upon the rocks, as is commonly believed; the well-known rock carvings being of a later and a ruder age. They used a polished slate, similar to that employed in our modern schools, the material being obtained in a hill to the north of the city of Phœnix. This was fashioned into convenient sizes, neatly squared and often ornamented around the edges, and probably inscribed by means of a pencil of the same material, or, in the case of permanent records, engraved with flint. While several of these slate tablets have been found in the ruins, no intelligible records have been discovered, nor could we expect otherwise, considering the nature of the material. The author heard of only one instance to the contrary, and then the tablet was accidentally destroyed before it could be submitted to scientific exam-

ination.   He was informed that the characters had the
general appearance of Chinese writing.

It is strange that they appear to have made no use of
the metals abundant in the vicinity, gold, silver and copper, and it has been assumed that there was some superstition against their use.

They possessed considerable engineering skill, shown
by the manner in which their canals keep steadily to the
line of their gradient.

They cremated the majority of their dead, burying
the ashes in earthen jars in family cemeteries, but en-
tombment was practised in some cases, many skeletons
having been found neatly walled up within the larger
houses.   Several of these were removed to the Smith-
sonian Museum in Washington, and an examination of
them shows that the ancient people were of tall stature,
and their skull formation not inferior to the best type
of Caucasian.

Having thus given a brief resumé of facts made
known by the ruins themselves, some account of the
earliest European explorers will be interesting.

Father Chino explored the Salt River valley at the
end of the seventeenth century, and found the Pima and
Maricopa tribes of Indians living in comfortable and
well constructed houses, their villages being located on
the *mesas* near the banks of streams, and well arranged
for defense.

The people were frugal and industrious and engaged

in cultivating the soil. They had irrigating canals, and the better class lived in *adobe* houses. They made cloth from a species of *maguey* and manufactured beautiful feather-work which was colored by means of dyes, the preparation of which was secret. There were among them adepts in hieroglyphic or picture writing, the significance of which was fully understood by a few.

Father Sedalman visited the same section in 1740. He described the mound at Tempe and gave an account of a three-story building found at the junction of the Gila and Salt rivers.

Fathers Pedro Font and Francisco Garcés explored the same country in 1795 and concluded that the ancient dwellers were the progenitors of the Aztecs, if not identical with them.

J. R. Bartlett, of the Boundary Commission, visited the Gila and Salt River valleys in 1850-1 and gave a minute account of his observations.

He made a careful examination of the ruins near the present sites of Phœnix and Tempe, and found ancient canals, mounds and broken pottery scattered through the valley. Several mounds measured eighty by one hundred and twenty feet, and that at Tempe, two hundred and twenty-five feet in length by eighty in width, showing that it was a much larger edifice than that at Casa Grande, which he also visited and described.

Twenty years ago there were abundant evidences of prehistoric habitation, and as the appearance of the ruins is now much changed, owing to general settlement, the following description written at the time is interesting:

"Six miles out of Phœnix are the ruins of a large town, in the center of which is a mound thirty feet high, two hundred and seventy-five feet long and one hundred and thirty feet wide; the walls stand about ten feet high and are six feet in thickness. There are evidences of several cross walls, and the whole was surrounded by an outer wall. On the north, and at the north-west corner were two wings, probably watch-stations or towers. On the south of the outer wall was a moat that could be flooded with water from a large reservoir, fifty yards away. There were several other large reservoirs at different points in and around the main town, which was over two miles in extent.

"A large irrigating canal, twenty-five to fifty feet wide, runs south of the main building, the water being conducted from the Salt river, eight miles above, and its course is traceable for over twenty miles below.

"The largest of the old irrigating canals begins twenty-five miles above Phœnix, on the south side of the Salt river, near the point where it emerges from the mountains, and for eight miles after leaving the river, it is fully fifty feet wide. For this distance its course is south-west until it reaches a vast stretch of level *mesa*, which extends south and south-westerly, thirty to sixty miles. The main canal here makes three branches, each twenty-five feet in width, and near the point of division are the vestiges of a town in the center of which are the ruins of the largest building yet discovered.

"Its ground measurement is three hundred and fifty by one hundred and fifty feet, not including outer walls, moats and embankments. The whole country under these canals is dotted with ruins, showing that many thousands of people once inhabited the valley, and carried the cultivation of the soil to a high state of perfection.

"In the Rio Verde valley there are evidences of a town with canals, ten miles from the nearest water, and buildings of solid masonry two stories in height, with walls three feet in thickness."

The foregoing facts will enable the reader to form some idea of the character of the prehistoric settlements, the grandest ruins of antiquity existing within the limits of the United States, and prepare his mind for the statement made upon the authority of reputable archæologists, that the Salt River valley alone must have sustained a population of not less than half a million of a people whose origin, name, language and characteristics, are utterly lost to the world.

A number of theories have been advanced to account for their disappearance. Drought, pestilence and the assaults of savage hordes have had their advocates, but neither has stood the test of criticism.

There is absolutely no proof that the climate has

CASA GRANDE RUINS.

The only thing remaining of a prehistoric race that once inhabited this country. These were ruins when discovered in 1540, so this country must have been inhabited when Columbus discovered America.

changed in the slightest degree, and conceding that it has not, the suggestion of pestilence is far-fetched.

The Apache Indians were never, so far as known, absolutely feared by the valley tribes existing to-day. They were dreaded, as many other pests might be, but the earliest settlers in Arizona remarked that the Pimas and Papagoes were able to offer effectual resistance to the savage marauders, and frequently compelled them to maintain peace for long periods. Hence, to impute to these nomadic savages the destruction of over five hundred thousand fairly civilized people, who well understood the arts of defense, is asking too much of our credulity.

The ruins of most of the forts or temples, located in the centers of populous districts, show that they were defended by walls, breastworks and even moats, and these could not have been intended for defense against undisciplined hordes of savages.

What man *has* done, that shall he do again,
  And in the interval, the ages run;
It is the eternal law, that nothing ends,
  Or only ends to be again begun!

    *   *   *   *

In the forgotten Past, these barren plains
  Nouirished a nation on their fertile soil;
Cheered countless souls along the path of life,
  Or gathered them to rest, when spent with toil.

  Their destiny fulfilled, the ages sped,
    Till man again resumed the abandoned strife:
  Then, on the mouldering ruins of the Past,
    Arose the fabric of a higher life!

THE SKYSTONE

CHAPTER I

Where? Whither? Whence?
  Why should ye seek to know?
Once on a time, I'll say, these people lived!
  The hills still rise around the plain, the rivers flow
  To-day, as then—*and men are much the same!*

THE sun set in a blaze of glory!

The pale blue of the zenith merged into green as it touched the golden fleece and ruddy bars that crowned the western hills. In the east the purple mountains were shot with bright flashes of crimson.

But night hovered behind them; stole over the pine-clad crests and into the gulfs between the ridges, and far out into the valleys; while light and shadow chased each other over the plains, kissing the grass and trees.

The air was still and full of balmy fragrance, as if the hour of sunset evoked an incense from nature! The great vault of heaven grew duller; the green changed to saffron, the gold and orange to brown and grey, and the mountains saddened, blackened and disappeared.

Still hung upon the highest peaks of the western hills, a faint tint of glory, the reflection of the sunrise of another world; but in a few moments this too faded, and the earth slept under a jeweled canopy!

*   *   *   *   *   *   *   *

Through the long day, a company of travelers traversed the valley of the Red Rocks in the direction of the land of Mázacl, with low ranges of tawny hills on each side, a chain of lofty mountains at their backs, and a scorching sun above them. As night fell, they halted by a grove of mesquite trees at the base of an isolated peak of peculiar shape, that rose like a sentinel at the western end of the valley where it opened out upon a vast plain.

There were twoscore men, about half of them being bearers of burdens, and when the command to halt was given, these latter unloosened their packs from their shoulders, and placing them upon the ground, squatted beside them and devoured their simple meal of ground corn and seeds, moistened with water from their gourds.

The balance of the party encamped about fifty paces to the west, and after building a fire prepared a more pretentious meal. It was evident from their dress and bearing that these were of a different race, for while the packbearers were flat featured and dark and wore only short tunics of coarse fibre cloth, these were clad in garments of cotton confined at the waist by belts of leather and were of nobler stature and features, and lighter of color.

They wore their hair worked into neat braids that hung down their backs, and bore arms of different kinds. After satisfying their hunger, they stretched themselves upon the ground and gazing at the ruddy embers of the fire listened to one who stood erect in their midst, as if scorning fatigue. His tall form stooped beneath the weight of years, but there was energy in his voice and fire in his eyes as he spoke in a low measured tone.

"We are now," he said, "at the eastern gate of the land of Mázacl, the dwelling of the Skystone! Yonder peak, the Axehead, as it is called, whose summit is crowned with stars, whose shadow at morning is in Mázacl and at evening darkens a foreign soil, marks the eastern bound of the Dominion of the lords of the Yellow Disk. Beyond live the wandering tribes, the Hillsmen, and the Tankmen!

"To-morrow our evening fire shall burn by the great lake of Ilome, and ere the sun sinks again into the great western sea, we shall behold the bright temple of Yahvan in a field of green and gold."

"What thinkest thou, lord Naqua, will be our reception there?" enquired one near him.

"No frost had touched my beard, and these withered limbs were supple and sinewy as a panther's when I last breathed the air of Mázacl, and Time worketh many

changes; yet it will be strange if there is not some re-
membrance of him who restored health to the lord
Huema when he lay dying of the shaking sickness! I
had trafficked from the Breasts of Coyoa to the north of
the inner sea, and came at last to the border of the land
of Mázacl, which I could not pass, being a stranger.
I heard of the illness of the lord Huema and I sent him a
few drops of an elixir prepared in the far south by a
people who live in trees, like apes, because for half the
year stagnant waters cover the earth, and huge monsters sport in the slime.

"It restored him to health and won me his friendship,
and by most solemn acts was I made free of the land,
to come and go, I and mine.   Should there be none to
know me, I have the yellow signet which he gave me,
and he, himself, showed me the secret of the symbols
of the sages, whereby I can make my thoughts known
at a distance, or read the thoughts of others.   Have no
fear, for they will surely breathe upon us in love and
friendship, and even though the Skystone escape us, yet
from our trafficking we shall return enriched.

"Beware though, of giving offence, for they are a
proud people, descendants of the yellow-skinned gods
who came from the home of the sun; came upon the
backs of white-winged birds across the endless waters,
as our own legends tell, for though they know it not,
we are of their kindred.   They are jealous of their customs and their gods.   With them the yellow metal is

ANCIENT CLIFF HOUSE, CASA GRANDE.

sacred to the sun-god, the white to the moon-god, and the red to the earth-god; therefore they shall not be used except in the service of the gods. Hide ye then what ye bear of these, that they be not provoked!

"Their women are pleasant of countenance, fair as the morning twilight, and have great eyes that ensnare the souls of men. Be ye blind to their charms and deaf to the music of their voices, sweeter than the song of the seashell; and taste not the honey of their lips. Neither prove ye the wine of Mázacl, which they drink at their feasts and merrymakings, for it is a wizard that changeth man's spirit. These two, women and wine, are the curse of great enterprises, and betray even the gods! Remember what we seek, and the oath that we have sworn to those who wait for us below the Breasts of Coyoa. The Skystone will turn back the curse that lies upon our land, and ye will be the greatest among our people, if ye succeed.

"I have spoken these words upon the edge of the land, for your guidance. Be wise and remember them. The night is growing old and weary limbs need rest! See thou, Tzihn, that the camp is well guarded and the slaves sleep by their packs. Let three at a time count the stars while an hour-stick burns; the rest to slumber!"

"I," said he called Tzihn, "will be of the first watch, for thou hast so filled my heart, that I should woo sleep in vain!"

"Thy wish is granted. Choose two others and be watchful!"

While the rest composed themselves to slumber, Tzihn and the two selected tied their long braids into knots upon their heads, armed themselves with javelins and bucklers, and lighting short punk sticks at the fire, plunged into the shadow. After making a careful round of the camp, each took his station, and the post of Tzihn ,was upon a rock, hurled from the summit of the cliff, whence he commanded an unobstructed view of the neighborhood, the bright starlight enabling him to distinguish objects to a considerable distance. He leaned upon the hilt of his javelin and peered hither and thither, and the hills across the pass appeared to come nearer as he gazed, and the stars hung in the middle air. As the moments sped, his form grew less rigid; his hands slid down the javelin until he rested upon the rock, and the stars danced before his eyes like fireflies!

There was a noise of moving stones, like the shaking of a gourd when the dancers roll it on the ground, but he heard it not. He opened his eyes and looked at his stick of punk and saw that it was burning low.

How tired he was! Thank the gods, it was about time to call another to take his place! He started to rise, but before he gained his feet, his arms were pinioned, and in a moment he lay gagged and bound, seeing nothing but the mocking stars, and hearing nothing but the rugged beating of his own heart!

* * * * * * * *

Naqua and those with him were sleeping heavily, so that dreams came not to them. About the end of the first watch, a creature, like an ape, entered the circle of light about the failing fire and surveyed the sleepers. Then it visited each in turn, and came at last to Naqua.

It felt his long white beard and fumbled about his neck until it touched a chain of turquoise to which was attached an oblong stone. With a low chuckle of pleasure, the creature unloosened this and hid it in its shaggy hair, and then ambled off into the shadow whence it came.

Dreams came to Naqua now!

A hideous monster sat upon his breast and held him spell-bound with its green, flaming eyes while it clawed at his beard. The eyes changed from green to yellow and from yellow to green, a green that blazed like a great meteor, and he knew that they were the Sky-stones; that which was lost and that which still shone in the holy chamber of Yahvan!

The mystic luster of the fateful gem, which had rested upon the breast of a god, paled as he looked until it became a white mist, which wound about him like a python, so that he felt his life going from him. The white curse of Coyoa had followed him! He cried to the gods and struggled fiercely—and awoke!

A human form crouched beside him with one sinewy hand about his throat, under his beard, and the other resting heavily upon his chest. A yellow face and great eyes, with a crest of tangled hair, hung over his own, as calm and passionless as that of a stone image. Each stared at the other while one could count a score; then Naqua's visitor drew back his head, and another figure showed in the dim light. A man of stalwart form clad in a *corium* or jacket of leather, below which fell the skirt of a tunic of some white material. Upon his head was a helmet or cap formed of the head of a lion, and about his neck a gorget from which hung a disc of gold as large as the palm of a man's hand; and when Naqua saw this symbol he knew that the wearer was a lord of Mázacl, and his fears subsided.

The stranger signed to his follower to step back, and adressing Naqua said: "If thou knowest the tongue of Mázacl, tell me who thou art, and thine errand here."

"Lord," answered Naqua in the same language, "I speak the tongue of Mázacl as thou hearest. I, and those with me, come from the south where the mountains pierce the clouds and the great cross of Azzua illumines the midnight sky. We are come to do homage to the lords of Mázacl, and to traffic with them and their people."

"Truly, thou speakest our tongue! Where didst thou learn it?"

"Even in the land of Mázacl, from the lips of the lord Huema, whose life I saved, when he lay dying of the shaking sickness."

The stranger paused a moment, and waved his hand towards the dark bushes to his right as if signaling to his followers.

"Thy name?"

"My lord's servant is called Naqua, and his sign is the Eagle."

"How shall I know that thou art not here for evil? Traffickers come not to Mázacl by the valley of the Red Rocks for a generation, for it has been forbidden to them."

"This I knew not, but my lord hears me speak with the tongue of truth."

"He who seeks to profit by falsehood, aptly uses the language of truth the better to accomplish his ends. Our slaves are liars; yet they use our tongue; and some of them have, perchance, strayed to thy land, and from them thou hast learnt."

"Among thy people are those who have breathed upon my face, after the custom of Mázacl, and by solemn acts was I made free of the land, I and mine. I can show, my lord, that I am no mere trafficker if he will lend me a tablet from his girdle."

The stranger drew forth from his pouch a tablet of slate and stylus of the same material and handed them to Naqua.

"What will my lord, that I write?"

"I swear, by my gods, that there is no guile in my heart."

Naqua approached near to the fire and proceeded to slowly outline the appropriate symbols, halting frequently, as if the art, though known, was unfamiliar from long disuse. When he had finished, he returned the tablet and stylus and stood with bowed head.

"Thou hast done well, but not faithfully, for thou hast written: 'I swear by the gods, that my heart is clean!'"

"My lord will consider that I am old and the memory of age is treacherous. If more proof is necessary, I have the yellow signet of lord Huema, which he gave me when we parted a generation ago."

So saying, he reached into his bosom and felt for the signet, and not finding it at once, he removed a chain of turquoise from about his neck, and saw that the stone was missing.

Vainly he sought it about his person, and upon the ground where he had slept, but found it not, and in his grief he beat his chest and pulled at his grey beard.

"I have lost the precious signet!" he cried, "or it has been stolen from me while I slept. Yet none knew its resting place but myself!"

The stranger smiled at his grief and approaching him, laid a hand upon his shoulder and bade him be comforted.

"I have heard the lord Huema speak of thee. He lives and thou shalt see him. Forgive me, if I have appeared to doubt thy truth, but much has happened since thou didst last set foot on the soil of Mázacl, to make us wary of admitting strangers. Betake thee now to rest, and at sunrise I will send thee a message and a guide. My warriors await me with impatience, and the sun must find us far away!"

The strange disturber of Naqua's slumber now returned and whispered in the ear of his lord and together they walked into the darkness.

While Naqua pondered over the visitation, and tried to account for the disappearance of the signet, a shrill whistle brought his sleeping companions to their feet, and Tzihn rushed among them, calling them to arms. But Naqua stayed them with a gesture and told them of the visit he had received, and then addressing Tzihn, said: "If thou hadst been vigilant, thou hadst seen them before I. Hereafter remember, that ears and eyes must not sleep when our trust is in them, if we would win the Skystone!"

Tzihn hung down his head and was silent.

CHAPTER II

The great designs of men are built on sand,
The sport alike of truant wind and flood:
Ambition's flight, the power of vigorous will,
Obey the uneven currents of the blood.

"Journey westward to the river; thence to the stony hills. Ilome is no more. I send thee a guide. Beware the Tankmen, their harvest has failed. I greet thee."

When the first grey light of morning dimmed the stars, a tablet bearing symbols of the above import was handed to Naqua by a hunchback of strange appearance.

An immense head, covered with long and tangled hair surmounted a body that was nearly all shoulders. His muscular arms almost touched the ground as he stood erect and his legs were like two bows. His height was about five feet, his color a tawny yellow like the skin of an antelope, and his countenance would have been forbidding but for the large, lustrous eyes, soft as a fawn's.

"This is a monster!" thought Naqua, "and should have been strangled at birth!" Then he asked him: "How art thou called?"

The hunchback picked up a stick of iron-wood of an

arm's length and as thick as a beam, and broke it across his shoulders as if it had been an arrow-shaft; and Tzihn remembered the assault of the night and wondered not that he had been helpless in such arms, and Naqua felt again the clutch upon his throat when he awoke from his dream!

"I am sometimes called the Bison of Mázacl, but to my lord the Lionhead, I am Tote."

"We will copy after thy lord, and call thee by that name, and if thou servest us faithfully, thou shalt be well recompensed."

"I serve only the Lionhead!" muttered Tote, and he sat down and ran his claw-like hands through his hair as if the people no longer interested him.

Naqua deciphered the message slowly again, for he understood not the allusion to Ilome, and when he asked Tote for light upon the subject, the hunchback gave him no answer, and he judged that some evil had befallen this people, whereof it was not lawful to speak.

Then seeing that his followers were impatient to learn the import of the message, he read it to them, and told them that the Tankmen referred to were dangerous savages that roamed over the arid plains south of Mázacl.

"They make tanks in the ground which catch the water when it rains and supply them during the dry seasons. They live on seeds, roots and game, depending upon the bounty of the clouds for one meagre crop of corn each year. If this fails them, as it often does, they become desperate and raid the outlying settlements. Under the impulse of hunger they are ravening beasts with the cunning of foxes, and now that their harvest has failed we must be careful for our safety. Let us prepare to move swiftly. Thou, Caluyo, art fleet of foot and shalt precede us three arrow-casts, to warn us of danger. Remember what I commanded with respect to metals, for we shall soon be in the midst of Mázacl!

"Lord Naqua," argued Tzihn, "if we remove the metal from our spears and javelins, they will be pointless, and in case of attack we shall be at great disadvantage."

"Have ye not flinted arrows and toothed clubs, besides the experience of tried warriors to counterbalance what ye lack in this respect? It must be so, for should we make what these people consider a sacrilegious use of a metal that has even the appearance of that which is sacred, even in defense of our lives and property, we shall be condemned—for such is the law. Nor is it such a great matter, for the Tankmen use not the bow and arrow, so little advanced are they in the art of war."

*   *   *   *   *   *   *   *

After three hours' journeying they beheld a ribbon of green crossing the plain in front of them, which marked the course of the stream that flowed between the Axehead and the Stony Hills. The approach from the east was over a short stretch of sand, dotted with red patches of a species of dock and brown clumps of dwarf mesquite.

Caluyo had passed the sand without observing any sign of danger, and paused at the stream to drink and refill his gourd.

Looking back, he saw the cavalcade reach the edge of the sand stretch, the hunchback in the lead, the slaves with their packs fifty paces behind the rest.

Tote stopped suddenly and raised his great head and sniffed the air like an alarmed antelope. Then he waved his long arms calling a halt.

He saw Naqua and Tzihn and the rest gather around, and while they talked excitedly, Tote pointed to the right, whence the wind came.

It was evident that Naqua saw no cause for alarm and resolved to proceed, but with more caution; and as they moved forward slowly, Tote drew off to one side and squatted upon a hillock, folding his arms over his knees. They had not advanced more than fifty paces when the ground appeared to rise up under their feet, the air was filled with sand and dock leaves, and threescore of naked savages were among them!

Caluyo flew back like an eagle, and plunged into the thickest of the fray, killing three of the savages before he sank upon the sand, the lifeblood oozing from a dozen gaping wounds.

Bows and arrows were flung aside, and Naqua and

his men fought with their clubs, save only Tzihn who had replaced the metal point upon his javelin.

But Tote remained where he had seated himself. He combed his hair with his long fingers and swung his body from side to side keeping time to a low chant. He saw a portion of the savage band cut off the bewildered slaves and drive them southward at the spear's point.

He saw the tall form of Naqua tower like a dry *saguara* in the midst of his warriors, and every minute a swarthy body shuddered beneath his toothed club; and by his side was Tzihn opening springs of blood with his javelin.

Fifteen of the enemy lay prostrate on the sand like the shadows of those that still stood, but there remained only one other with Naqua and Tzihn!

Three against a dozen!

The savages now prepared for the last move, that would leave none alive to tell the story, for Tote, with his hair falling about him, looked so much like a dry bush, that he was not perceived.

Naqua leaned for a moment upon the shoulder of Tzihn and muttered a prayer to the gods, and Tzihn looked up at him and smiled!

In the sullen silence, more enervating than the fray, they heard nothing but the beatings of their own hearts, and the cracking of their breath.

The savages circled about them drawing nearer at every revolution.

Nearer and nearer they pressed, making fierce lunges with their gory spears, and throwing sand in the faces of their prey.

Blinded and fainting with fatigue, the three had heart and strength to turn the spears aside or receive them on their leather bucklers, but many were drawn back weeping blood, and when this happened, the savages yelled with exultation.

Having thus weakened them by intimidation, they made a simultaneous rush. There was a rattle of wood and short thuds of blows, cries of agony and gasps of dying breath, and when the assailants drew off again, Naqua and Tzihn were alone.

Two against six!

They stood only long enough to see the great universe gyrate about them, and then they sank upon their knees, and Tote saw two blood-stained faces, eyes dull with agony, and a javelin and a club trembling in the nerveless hands that held them.

The white beard of Naqua had turned to brown and he and Tzihn were naked above the waist.

Tote gathered his hair into a knot upon his head, and crawled towards them upon the sand.

When the savages advanced to finish their work, he sprang upon them from behind, and with one sweep of his long arms pulled two to the earth with such suddenness and force that they were stunned.

A third thrust at him wildly with a spear, but he

seized it in midair and broke it as if it had been a dry twig.

Before they could recover from their astonishment, he took the club from the palsied hand of Naqua and rushed upon them, snorting like an angry bear, and such was the strength of his long arm and the quickness of his eye that no defense availed against him, and in a few moments the last of the savages clutched at the hot sand, digging his own grave!

Then Tote sat down and unfastened his hair, and looked towards the south!

CHAPTER III

Tzihn opened his eyes, and saw above him an endless row of rafters with deep shadows between, and this puzzled him so much that he fell asleep and dreamed that he was in the pine forests of his native mountains, looking up at the barred sky. When he awoke again, he saw nothing, for it was dark. The darkness oppressed him and he tried to rise, but his head was heavy and his limbs so stiff that he could not move.

Where was he?

His throat was parched and he called for water in a voice so feeble that it sounded like the whine of an infant. A ray of light danced along the rafters, and the face of a spirit, more beautiful than the loveliest daughters of earth, with eyes that shone like the evening star, and lips that opened like a flower heavy with dew, hung above his own and seemed to draw out his soul through his eyes.

He had reached the home of the gods, where celestial maidens receive the souls of the dead!

A soft hand crept under his head, now shorn of its locks, and raised it so that he could drink the nectar which would revive his spirit after its long journey from earth. He drank slowly, gazing into those eyes, and when he had finished, his soul was drowned in their depths!

When he next awoke, the light of an earthly day was about him, and he knew that he still lived.

But what of Naqua, and the rest?

The rest! Ah, he remembered them now—strewn about him upon the sand, the shadows of those that had been—and the tears came to his eyes. They had gone down like trees before the flood when the windows of heaven are open and the clouds break upon the hills. The noblest and bravest of Coyoa. His friends and brothers; and he alone was left! He strove to turn so that he could bury his head in his arms and weep for the dead, but a firm hand held him still, and he looked up and saw the white beard of Naqua!

"Peace, Tzihn! It is I that am with thee. Seven long days and nights hast thou wrestled with the death-god, but thy youth hath driven him back to the middle air, and thou shalt live. Thou canst not rise yet, my son, but good friends have thee in charge, and I am with thee. Since it is harmful for thee to talk, I will allay thy curiosity. Thou wast wounded almost to death, but Tote, the hunchback, saved us—thee and me—the rest were called by the gods! The lord Lionhead had missed our

MOQUI OR ZUNI PUEBLIO, CASA GRANDE.

assailants, but encountered those that drove off our slaves, and guessing what had befallen us, hastened to our rescue. He came too late to save our brethren. Their bodies rest by the side of the river; their spirits are above the clouds. The gods decreed that the glory should not be divided. Thou alone must save our people—for Naqua is like a dead tree, fit only to feed the fire. Thou and thine will reap the reward, and in the time to come, the memory of Naqua will be a dream in the hearts of his people! Thou wouldst ask a question?"

"The daughter of a god has been with me."

A shadow crossed the face of his friend, as he replied to the half exclamation and half interrogation of the sick man: "Thou hast been dreaming! No one has been with thee but I, and Tote and a servant of the temple. Compose thyself to slumber again, for sleep is the balm thou needest, and if the spirit come not to thee again, it shall be a sign that the gods are friendly!"

He pressed his cool hand upon the patient's brow and held it there until he slept again.

With a sigh of relief, he passed out of the chamber into an open court wherein grew trees and flowering plants in great profusion, and as he entered it, there came towards him from the opposite side, a young woman of striking beauty, but haughty mien. Her well-rounded form was robed in a white garment of cotton, gathered about her waist by a girdle of rich feather-work.

Naqua muttered to himself: "This is the spirit of Tzihn's dreams. It is an evil spirit for him and must be banished!"

They met about midway of the path across the court, and Naqua bowed low as he said: "The lady Zaca is more potent than the physician, for she adds a virtue of her own to his simple remedies that gives them miraculous power. In a few days my friend will be like a young wolf, full of hunger and love of freedom. His weakness will be his shame and even now he chafes at confinement, and snarls at his friends!"

The lady Zaca frowned. "Adversity," she said, "has made me quick-witted, and I know that thy words are rich in meaning. They are like the smoke of a fire. Why veil thy thoughts from the daughter of a smitten race, kept like a caged bird to teach the children patience! Let the wisdom of thy years proclaim itself freely."

"The wisdom of man, lady, is weak compared to the darting intuition of woman, which has the eye of an eagle, and the swiftness of a panther. Between us there shall be no mystery. My brother is of a warm-blooded race, and thou art the fairest of the daughters of earth. Thou hast already possessed his dreams, and the reality, if he see it, will far exceed his visions, and what is palpable stimulates desire. Such a passion will destroy him, for he is a stranger and cannot, lawfully, raise his eyes to thee. I thought of this when the lord Lionhead urged thy wonderful power over disease and wounds."

"The lord Naqua need have no fear! My compassion is for the suffering alone. Now that thy friend is well, he hath no need of me, nor I of him!" and she turned aside with a smile and sat down by a pool of water in the center of the court.

Naqua stroked his beard and looked after her with a puzzled air, and thought, "If a man should live a thousand years, he could not comprehend a woman!"

And Zaca while she gazed upon her fair face reflected in the pool, said to herself: "A woman's will is stronger reason than the sage's wisdom. No stranger's eye can gaze upon a daughter of Mázacl to woo her! Am I not a stranger too? Despised yet entertained, more feared than loved; the memory of a crime, the spirit of a vengeance sleeping, but not dead!"

   *   *   *   *   *   *   *   *

Leaving the court, Naqua passed through a narrow passage that opened upon the bank of a canal fringed with trees, and beyond the trees rose the temple of Yahvan.

The temple was in reality an agglomeration of buildings rising gradually to a center, giving the effect of a pyramid. The outer walls were faced with stucco or fine cement, the material being sun-burnt brick. The first and second course of buildings were of a dull red tint, the next was white, and the fourth yellow; the three colors symbolizing the religious emblems of the earth, the moon and the sun respectively. Around the whole mass of buildings was a deep fosse, which could be flooded at will from an adjacent reservoir; between the fosse and the buildings was an escarpment faced with stone, and beyond this a low wall of sun-dried brick.

The general effect was impressive, notwithstanding the rudeness of the material, and the lack of architectural or even orderly arrangement.

To Naqua the temple had ceased to be a wonder, and perhaps, it never was such to one who had seen the great pyramids and temples of the south. He ascended the escarpment, still meditating deeply, and entered the structure through a doorway used only by familiars of the temple, and from a chamber of moderate dimensions ascended, by means of a ladder to another of greater size wherein were men engaged in different occupations.

Addressing one of them who wore a girdle of yellow cloth he bade him inform the lord Huema that his servant, Naqua, awaited his pleasure.

The man departed, and returning in a few moments, conducted him through several chambers to one of considerable size, wherein a man of advanced age, with a beard of two spans' length, sat upon a rush mat, writing with a stylus upon a slate. As the visitor approached, he arose, and meeting him, placed his hands upon his shoulders and breathed gently upon his face.

"Peace to thee, and welcome, Naqua! How dost thy friend?"

"Thy friend's friend is doing well, and with a few more days of rest will be able to walk in the sunlight and drink in the wonders of Yahvan!"

"Thou art an excellent physician."

"I deserve not all the credit. The lady Zaca has more skill than I."

"She learnt the mysteries of herbs from her foster mother, Popoche, whose skill was marvelous, but thy modesty gives her more than her due."

"I have prided myself upon my skill."

"Thy travel has given thee more experience than usually falls to the lot of man, and upon this depends the skill of the physician. We are duller in these matters. Like a still pond, we reflect the same trees and skies, day after day. The dry leaves fall upon us; the winds ruffle our surface, and as the years pass we grow shallower. We travel little or not at all, and we know even less than our fathers. Custom has built a wall about us, and superstition keeps it in repair or adds to its height. Those who pass the barriers see more and their knowledge has the element of wonder to those who live forever behind them."

"But in recompense for these material things, thou hast that, Lord Huema, which is more important to man than the prolongation of his life. We, who live beyond the walls, pass through life, gathering the bitter and the sweet, heedless of whence they come and what they mean; whilst thou touchest the origin of things, and lookest into the heart of the mysteries that appal our minds, when we pause to think! Life is the shadow of a bird in flight; away flies the bird, and then there is neither bird nor shadow! If that we live only to die, he is a curse to man who bids him live, for death brings rest.

"Out of thy great knowledge thou teachest differently. The soul of man is a bird in flight; life is its shadow cast upon the earth which disappears because the bird flies home!

"O thou, who canst lift the veil, let Naqua see beyond!"

Lord Huema sighed heavily and shook his head: "Beyond the darkness is a darkness more profound!" and conducting his visitor to the mat where he had risen, bade him be seated.

Taking up the tablet upon which he had been writing, he read:

"Who seeketh knowledge for the enlargement of his soul is greater than a prophet!

"Believe not in thyself till the day of thy death.

"Prepare thyself in the ante-chamber that thou mayst gain admittance to the holy place.

" 'Man cometh into the world with his hands

clenched, as if he could grasp all things and he leaveth it with his hands open, for what he hath grasped has slipped away:' These are jewels of thought; stars in the firmament of wisdom. They are the wisdom of the ancient sages, not my own; the kernels of truth that show us wherein we should strive most; yet to youth they are sayings that hang on hairs!"

Then laying the writing aside, he placed one hand upon Naqua's knee and said: "Thou didst render me a service for which my gratitude is scant recompense, for thou didst prolong a life, which, had it ended there, were incomplete, unsatisfied and vain. I stood upon the threshold of the wisdom of the ancients, but my soul was full of error. Thou didst remain with me until thy knowledge of our tongue was nearly perfect. I taught thee the symbols of light, and in exchange for lessons from thy experience, showed thee many things that were strange to thee. Hadst thou stayed longer, I might have done more; but—" and the speaker paused and looked at Naqua intently for a moment "—thy heart yearned for thy people and kindred, and I bade thee go in peace, and gave thee my signet to remind thee that thou shouldst come again. Was it not thus?"

Naqua bowed his head.

"Thou hast returned as I wished; but thy hair is like the tops of the hills in winter. Age has sown thy face with grey hair, and thy blood is cool as a mountain stream. In middle age thou wert apt, but then the mind is still like the outer walls of the temple; it lightens in the sunlight, and when the sunshine goes, it has no memory of it. But the light of truth abides with age. Youth and manhood seek only for signs, and their hopes and fears follow them like their own shadows. Thou art now ripe for knowledge, for the end of the journey makes the road seem short. For thee ambition's goad has no point, glory is madness and the eyes of love as lusterless as dead pearls. If it can be done I will lead thee where no stranger feet have ever trodden, and crown thy days with peace!

"The feast of the harvest draws nigh when the Great Council meets, and if thy desire is still steadfast, I will bring the matter before them."

Naqua kissed the speaker's robe and clenched his hand as one who struggles with his soul. He knew that before he could penetrate the mysteries of the temple, he must pretend to become a citizen of Mázacl. The matter now, as once before, seemed easy enough from afar, as the distant hills are smooth as the cheek of a girl until approached, when rugged rocks and chasms dark appear. But he had sworn to do it, and Tzihn was left, free to wander back to the Breasts of Coyoa, and bear the treasure to his people. He would remain to suffer as the gods willed!

"Lord Huema," he said, "the rush of my life is over. I have outlived those that were dear to me and am alone

—alone with my soul! My father brought me into the world, but thou shalt lead me out of it into eternity."

And lord Huema smiled and blessed him.

CHAPTER IV.

Upon the sun-lit surface of the pool,
  The trees and sky in mystic beauty lie;
But when the sun behind the clouds retires,
  The sullen pool, shows neither trees nor sky.

"Cousin Tote, move my seat into the shade, for see, the sun falls upon me!"

Tote was stretched upon the ground, holding up his giant head with his large hands, drinking in the beauty of the lady Zaca, who sat by the pool in the court.

She was sewing a garment with a needle made of a fish-bone and a thread spun in the temple from the soft cotton grown below the red cliffs by the Two-Waters.

Tote sprang to his feet, agile as a monkey, and moved the seat, with as much reverence as if it had been the throne of a goddess. Then he returned to his worship.

"Why devourest thou me with thy great eyes?"

"Thou art so beautiful, cousin Zaca, that it refreshes my soul to do so."

"And thou art so ugly that if thou didst gaze upon the pond, the surface would ruffle with affright! And yet, if thou wast like other men, I believe I should like thee less."

"Dost thou hate other men?"

"I do not love them."

"Not even the lord Lionhead, who has cared for thee as his sister."

"Shall I love the enemies of my people?"

"I love him."

"It is thy fancy, because he is kind. Thou art to him a tame wolf. Thy uncouth form ennobles his; thy shortness adds to his stature; thy great strength supplements his dexterity; thy subservience flatters his vanity. In his heart thou art a slave even as I am!"

He combed his hair and looked so sad and puzzled that Zaca laughed.

"Thou wilt hate me for the bitter words I speak. Since Popoche left me thou art my only friend, and upon thee I must outpour the bitterness of my spirit or it will consume me!"

"I cannot help but love thee, for thou art beautiful and my cousin."

"Dost thou love all that is beautiful?"

"I cannot help it. I love the flowers, the sunlight and the stars, the birds and butterflies, the towering mountains and the endless plain, the melodies I hear and those that come to me in dreams, but most of all I love that which makes sweet music in my soul!"

"Knowest thou one more beautiful than I?"

He closed his eyes and said: "While I see thee I cannot think, but now thou art shut out, I see a face, poor, pinched and wan, and yet it has a beauty thou hast not, which when I see, the music of the gods sounds in my ear and lifts my spirit to the skies!"

"Where hast thou hidden this paragon?"

"In my heart! She is a child—ask me no more, for see, I look on thee again. Why cannot we love all that is good! Why shouldst thou hate my lord? Should the wrongs done to our fathers poison our blood? He calls me brother, when his heart is at peace and, indeed, I love him. Why should we, being of the same blood, be so different—thou beautiful as a dream, and I as ugly as a toad?"

"Ask the lord Huema, for he knoweth all things from the gods. I only know that I live and am my father's child. How does the wounded stranger?"

Tote's eyes brightened at this change of the subject and he replied: "He fares well and gathers strength like a shoot of corn. In a few days thou shalt see him in the court."

"This is what I fear, for then I cannot enter it—and I so love the bright flowers, the whispering leaves and the pond!"

"He will not harm thee; and hast thou not saved his life?"

"His eyes were soulless then; but now he sees as thou dost, and it is not proper that we should meet, for he is a stranger! Yet I love my seat here by the water under the trees, where the birds sing in the morning, and the cool shadows fall. Wilt thou not spare me this pleasure, and have him lodged elsewhere? Beyond my chamber is one that faces the temple. It is pleasanter than the one he has, and the trees upon the canal are tall and thick. If he were there, he would not seek the court!"

"But that is still nearer to thee!"

"And farther from the spot I love. Here I can sit and dream when I please, and gather flowers or sew. Here too thou canst come when thou art not following the Lionhead, and listen to my voice!"

"I will find some reason for making the change, since it is thy wish."

"I thank thee, cousin. What manner of speech has the stranger?"

"It sounds like our own."

"Thou shouldst teach him ours, and when he can speak it, have him tell thee of the wonders he has seen. I am weary of the eternal sameness here, and would hear of other lands and other lives, and thou canst repeat what he tells thee. If thou art faithful to thy word, I will weave thee a wreath of flowers for the feast of the harvest."

His eyes sparkled with delight, and he rose and shook himself, and there fell upon the ground a yellow stone, oblong in shape, and worked with strange symbols. He snatched it up quickly and sought to conceal it, but the lady Zaca caught his hand, and at her touch his great strength slept.

"What hast thou there?"

He hung his head in confusion.

She removed it gently from his grasp and examined it carefully.

"This is a strange talisman. The symbols have no meaning to me and yet they look like the symbols of thought."

He sought to take it back, but she pressed his hand aside, and hid it in her bosom.

"How camest thou by it?"

He tried to evade the question, but she pressed him so that he told her how he had taken it from Naqua while he slept at the base of the Axehead, thinking it must be a talisman of great power and in the possession of a stranger—perhaps an enemy—would work ill to the people of Mázacl.

"Thou didst well, and I will keep it for thee!"

*   *   *   *   *   *   *   *

Tzihn was removed upon Tote's suggestion, but the change was followed by complications that set Naqua's skill at defiance, and at the end of a week his life hung by a hair.

About this time too, the hunchback had to follow his lord in pursuit of the Tankmen, who, in the desperation of hunger had dared to ravage several outlying settlements, carrying off large quantities of corn and killing those that withstood them.

While he remained, he had faithfully reported the

sick man's condition to Zaca, who, strangely enough, appeared to grow lighter in spirits as the news became more doleful.

Naqua realized, as he stood by his comrade's couch, that he had reached the limit of his skill, and that the last connection between him and his people was dissolving like the mist of the morning.

Though his mind was above the common superstitions, he believed in evil spirits, and thought their influence was at work, a belief that was strengthened by the actions of Tzihn in his waking moments. He prated of the spirit that waked him in the night, and this could not be the lady Zaca, for since the conversation in the court she had not come near him. Had he been wise in exiling her?

Sleep was now the patient's normal condition, and that which should have meant rest and nerve building was a disease that bore him slowly to the grave.

And if he died, who would return to the Breasts of Coyoa; who could bear the Skystone thither and stay the curse? The whole fabric was falling—and Naqua groaned in agony of spirit.

A shadow darkened the doorway.

He raised his eyes and through the moisture that filled them, saw the lady Zaca standing upon the threshold.

About her form was a loose robe that looked as if it had been stripped from the breasts of a thousand birds, so silky was it and radiant of color! Her black hair, lightened by waves of blue, was bound with a string of shells upon a ribbon of cloth, and her fair neck was clasped with a chain of pearls and turquoise.

"I am come," she said, "because I heard that the lord Naqua's brother was passing away!"

He did not reply at once, for his mind was full.

All his skill had failed! This maiden, standing before him like a goddess, the white light giving an opalescent lustre to her cheek, and scintillating in her big eyes; her robe shimmering like the spray of a waterfall in the sunlight, her very form giving an impression of grace and power—was no ordinary woman, but a child of Nature's passion, half mortal and half spirit.

As the thunderbolt sometimes pictures an image upon what it strikes, so had hers been flashed upon the mind of his dying friend—burned in so deep that it was consuming his life!

Might not the presence of the realty drive out the phantasm and win him back to life?—and life has possibilities, while death has none.

Could he trust her! Yes—he would consider the saving of life first, and trust the gods for the rest!

"The lady Zaca is welcome, though she cometh in an evil hour, for the shadow of death falls on the wall. The gods have blessed thee with a healing hand and thou knowest the qualities of the herbs of Mázacl bet-

MOQUI OR ZUNI PUEBLIO, CASA GRANDE.

ter than I.   I pray thee forget what I have said to thee, and save him if thou canst."

Grief filled his eyes as he spoke and he saw not the flash of triumph in hers.

"The lord Naqua has but to command.   What he said is returned to him unspoken.   May the gods give me the power they have denied to age and wisdom!"

She bade him leave her alone with the dying man, and see that none entered the chamber, otherwise her powers were weakened.

Naqua paused upon the threshold and looked back at her.

She smiled upon him with the smile of an infant, and he left marveling, for his wisdom faltered before the light of her countenance.

She approached the couch and surveyed the sick man attentively; noted the waxen pallor of his face and the slow breathing like the voice of the wind when it rustles the dry leaves.   She lifted his arm and it fell limp and lifeless by his side.   An anxious expression came to her face and her hand trembled, for she had not expected to find the case so hopeless.   Repressing her fears, she hurried to the door and drew across it a curtain of fibre cloth that subdued the light without excluding it entirely.   Having done this, she crossed to the back of the chamber near the corner furthest from Tzihn's couch and pressed lightly against the wall.

It yielded to her touch, revealing a door formed of

woven twigs plastered with mud and cement, and hung upon a central pivot!

Through this opening she passed into her own chamber whence she returned quickly with a small jar of a liquid, whose pungent odor, when she uncovered it, filled the room.

"Now," she said, "to test the elixir of Popoche!"

Unwinding the upper fold of her robe, so as to leave her arms free, she anointed his face and bust, rubbing the flesh lightly but swiftly until her hands were numbed.

In the same manner she treated his arms and then covered up his head and chest with a thick robe.

Entering her chamber again through the wall she returned quickly with a small gourd whose contents she emptied into a vessel that had held water, and uncovering his head laved it with her hands after dipping them in the liquid.

She dried his face with a cloth and kneeling by his head pressed her hands against his temples and blew into his nostrils.

For a moment he ceased to breathe, and she shuddered!

Then his breath returned—first fitfully in short gasps ending in sighs, but it gathered strength until his chest rose and fell easily and the cool dew of health beaded his forehead.

She removed her hands, arose and drew back the cur-

tain so that a ray of light fell upon her where she stood
—a few paces from the couch—and Tzihn's eyes
opened, and he saw her!

Was she the phantom of his dreams, or a woman
with life and passions like his own!

He strove to speak, but his heart choked his voice,
and he gazed in silent ecstacy, feeding his soul, before
she faded away into the wall. But instead of disap-
pearing, the vision approached him, knelt by his side,
gathered his face into its hands and smiled upon him!
A subtle perfume, sweeter than the breath of flowers,
filled his nostrils, and his senses slept.

When they awoke she was there where he had seen
her first, and a strange magnetism stirred his blood, and
he knew that he should live. She placed a finger upon
his lips, and pointing to herself said: "Zaca!" and he
echoed back the word, knowing that it was the name
of the divine creature who had materialized to save
him.

He said "Tzihn!" and smiled with joy when she repeated it so sweetly that it was music in his ears; and
these two words "Zaca" and "Tzihn" passed between
them so often that the air was full of them!

She offered him water and bade him drink while she
pillowed his head upon her arm, but he would not taste
it until she had put it to her own lips.

Then he drank a nectar distilled for the gods!

* * * * * * * *

Thereafter Naqua came and saluted the lady Zaca; and the heart of Tzihn was glad, for now it was certain she was of the earth.

"I see that thou art better, my son.   Truly, the lady Zaca has the gift of hands and cunning skill!"

But the sick man only smiled at him, for his joy was too great for speech.

* * * * * * * *

His beautiful physician visited him thrice each day, and his recovery was rapid.

She taught him to use the tongue of Mázacl, and he learned swiftly, as a child.   In a little while he seemed to understand all that she said, although he expressed himself with difficulty.

At first he grieved when she was absent, but noting this, she rebuked him and thereafter he yielded no more to melancholy, but the passion of an absorbing love grew with returning strength, and she knew that the life she had given to him was hers.

And Naqua noted this, and it worried him.

CHAPTER V.

THE temple of Yahvan was the chief granary of Má-zacl as well as its religious, educational and political center, and at harvest-tide all the dwellers therein had much to do. Nevertheless, the lord Huema found time to instruct Naqua, and what he said was eagerly devoured, as crumbs from the table of wisdom.

He explained to him, the social and political maxims that governed the lives of the people, which though but the sayings of the sages, were in effect, their laws.

"At thy former visit," he said, "thou didst exchange thy wares on the border with our own merchants, for no foreign traffickers are permitted in the land. Our merchants bring their goods to the great market and then exchange them for such articles as they deem most serviceable to them.

"The interchange of commodities is a cumbersome system, and the freer use of certain gems and shells has been often suggested, but the employment of mere representatives of value has its disadvantages; men come to regard them as the things they symbolize and lose the substance for the shadow.

"Our own experience has been that men will hoard stones and shells to make them scarce with the people and thus enhance the value, so that what is the token of one measure of corn is able to purchase two. This is a result injurious to the common welfare, for no man, by the exercise of superior cunning, has a right to double the value of that which he possesses, at the expense of his neighbor.

"The fact that others have the same privilege, which has been advanced in its favor, is really an argument against it, for should every man devote his time and talents to the business of overreaching his neighbor, the social fabric would quickly dissolve, and we should become like wild-dogs, who are said to eat each other. The matter has another phase, showing that like all evil systems, it carries with it the seeds of its own corruption.

"When the fine shells become scarce and of great value, traffickers come with slaves laden with them alone, expecting to make great gains; but, behold, the shells cheapen so quickly, that what was equal to one measure of corn buys only one-tenth of the quantity, and the hoarders of shells, who hoped to rob their brethren have to beg food of them or come to the granaries ! Precious stones and pearls, being more difficult to get, are consequently more stable in value, but they lack the element of cheapness, and can never become popular with the vulgar, who will always prefer quantity to quality. The Great Council has been urged to place the seal of the temple upon certain approved tokens, basing their issue upon the stores of grain and seeds deposited in the granaries; but the plan was not seriously entertained, for those who urged it would be the first to denounce it as an unjust interference with their rights.

"The promoters of the scheme proposed that every man who wished to do so, should have the right to deposit his produce and receive therefor sealed tokens corresponding to its value, these being redeemable in the same produce on demand. Hence, in time of abundance, the tokens would have small value and be accumulated by those who had more cunning than their neighbors, and when the evil days came, the poor and the negligent would suffer, and the full granaries would mock their misery.

"I have, therefore, opposed the free use of tokens, holding that the ancient sages spoke wisely when they said: 'No man is entitled to that which belongs to another, who cannot offer something that he has, both things being useful or necessary, as the product of his labor. Cunning is not prudence, and commerce is an incident of social life and not its end. While exchange is difficult, men will be more satisfied with what they have, and contentment is the road to happiness!' Above all things, the food and raiment of the people should be placed beyond the reach of speculation. The law ordains that enough food shall be stored in the public granaries to protect the people from actual want from one season to another. Each family furnishes its quota, and if a favorable season or superior husbandry produces a surplus, this is disposed of at pleasure.

"A tithe is reserved for the expense of the common defence, the maintenance of the canals and the education of the children.

"The temple has its own lands and slaves, and is no public burden. We judge between those who have differences, and punish the malicious wrong-doer; we educate the youth, and instruct and direct the artificers. In all other matters the people are governed by their local councils, each of which is represented in the Great Council. Only those of the pure race can receive instruction in the temple, bear arms or become artificers. The slaves are not of our blood, being kindred of the Tankmen. When our fathers settled here they dwelt by the streams and raised crops on the flood-lands, and were constantly at war with their brethren of the plains. While I like not this matter of life bondage, it has the approval of antiquity and many natural and reasonable claims. The purest water will deposit a sediment, if left to stand, and the clearest pool has mud at the bottom. Society is like a pool of water; there may or may not be slime on the surface, but the bottom is ever foul.

If some men are not pressed down by their fellows, their own passions will sink them; hence, in any social organism there must be a sediment of debased humanity.

"Our fathers, in their wisdom, judged that it was better to have a sediment of bondsmen than of freemen, for the first can be restrained and the latter cannot. In the case of our slaves, ignorance and baseness are associated with loss of liberty and mean employment, and hence, every freeman is proud of being such, and out of this pride springs the safety of our institutions.

"Yet this moral consequence is not depended upon exclusively, for it is a law, that he who intermingles with a slave shall be cut off from our people, and the slave shall die. I have noted with some uneasiness, that the slaves increase in numbers more than their masters, and notwithstanding they have neither arms nor warlike arts, it is easy to conceive of a time when they may overwhelm us by sheer force of numbers. This matter has been discussed in the Council, but as the danger is remote, no resolution has been reached. Should it become serious, the remedy is very simple, but so inhuman that only extreme necessity could justify it.

"It is a law, as thou knowest, that no slave shall be taught any handicraft save one, and this, being a punishment, is abominated by them; hence they are dependent upon us for all the comforts they enjoy. We impose upon them no great hardships, and they appear to be as contented with their lot as the caged bird that has never aired its wings in freedom.

"Thou, who hast traveled much and seen many forms of government, wilt, perhaps, condemn a system which regards innovation as a crime, and say that we lose much by attempting no change; that men's minds become shallow when their lives are circumscribed by ancient custom. Yet license has its evils, and the bonds of custom once broken, passion more than reason, rules the minds of men. A generation ago, the land of Ilome was a fair garden, and we of Mázacl envied its people; but the evil days came when it departed from the customs of our forefathers.

"The lord Tzah, chief of the Council, was ambitious and visionary. From time immemorial, the Council of Ilome had been subordinate to that of Mázacl and his first step was to deny our supremacy and refuse to send delegates. They were our brethren, and we did not seek to coerce them. Then he abolished the Council and assumed the paramount authority; but his ambition grew with his success. He imputed to his own virtue that which proceeded from the indolence of a people averse to contention, and disposed to accept what the gods sent.

"From remote antiquity, the chief keeper of the temple of Yahvan has been regarded as the successor of the prophet of our race, and the custodian of the sacred writings and relics; but the lord Tzah, listening to evil counselors, denounced me as an usurper of the sacred office, and proclaimed himself the legitimate successor. He forbade his people to make their customary pilgrimages to Yahvan and sought to enforce his pretensions by threats and acts of hostility, making bad blood between our people and those of Ilome. I did all in my power to stay the strife, but my efforts were like fuel to the wild ambition of Tzah, and even angered my own people, whose fields were being wasted by their enemies. A fierce battle was fought, and the furrowed fields ran blood! The lord Tzah disappeared, and the leaders of his people were made outcasts and fled to the mountains. The great reservoirs of Ilome were dry, the canals filled with mud and weeds, nor were we numerous enough to care for them, for many perished in the war. And its fate has taught us that it is dangerous to unsettle men's minds."

CHAPTER VI

THE city of Yahvan covered, loosely, a considerable area, following the banks of the main canal.

A short distance to the south-west of the temple was an open square, called the Meeting-place, and to one side of it was a sunken amphitheater wherein were held the games and public exhibitions. At the west end of the amphitheater rose a pyramidal structure reserved for the use of the priests and sages. The canal crossed the great square upon the same side, and the market-place was under the shade of its trees.

The Feast of the Harvest began upon the first day of the full moon, when the crops had been gathered and garnered, and the husbandman was at liberty to turn his thoughts from labor. Not until the granaries were full, a portion for each man, woman and child, free and slave, ensuring to all a sure subsistence until the next harvest, were the people free to dispose of their surplus. This year the harvests had been abundant, and the merchants arranged their wares in the market-place, under the trees, in great good humor, knowing that business would be brisk and profitable.

As it was unlawful for a stranger to sell in Mázacl, the wares of Naqua and Tzihn, which had been recovered from the Tankmen, were placed in charge of men of the temple to be sold. These being of rare quality attracted the most attention for it was seldom that the products of the far south came to the land in such abundance and excellence.

There were cloths, plain and colored and worked with silk and feathers; woven hair and silk and fabrics of cotton and hemp; curious armor of leather and the scaly hides of river monsters; precious essences of herbs and flowers whereof a few drops were worth a measure of corn; nut oil and liquid amber, shells of strange shapes and beautiful colors, rubber balls and dyes. There were chocolate and dried fruits, quaint images of alabaster and onyz, ornaments of rich design, parrots that used human speech, and animals that only lacked this art to make them counterparts of man; fragrant and medicinal herbs, the fiery ginger root and sweet licorice; skins of beasts and birds; pearls, opals and a hundred articles for use or ornament.

There were stores of salt from beyond the great river; dried flesh of the bison and antelope, blankets of soft hair, robes, sea-shells and strange things like ferns and leaves, fashioned by men who live under the waters; corn-mortars from the black hills beyond the valley, of the Red Rocks, and articles of bone and horn, needles and combs for the housewives.

The artificers of the temple gave evidence of their great skill in arms and armor, implements of husbandry, wickerwork, mats, garments of cotton and fibre, pottery and leatherwork; while the husbandmen brought stores of grain and seed, nuts, chili, pulse, edible roots, onions, honey, preserves in jars and seed cakes. There were booths wherein the weary might rest and drink corn wine and mead and cool water from the jars, seasoned with herbs and flowers; wherein too, the hungry found fresh steaming corn-cakes and toasted flesh garnished with onions and chili.

During the first day of the feast, none bought or sold, but each examined his neighbors' stocks and formed a proximate estimate of the condition of the market, whereby to regulate his own demands.

On the morning of the second day, before yet the dawn had been proclaimed from the summit of the temple, the market-place was thronged, with here and there a yellow girdled officer of the temple whose duty it was to preserve order and settle disputes. While the shadows of the trees were long, the slaves bustled hither and thither bearing burdens, and before the noon hour the stocks of many of the merchants had changed character several times.

There was busy hum and movement. Ejaculations of disappointment and shouts of delight resounded

upon all sides, as some unfortunate failed to secure a
coveted article, or another acquired the object of his
desire. There was merry laughter when one who had
bartered several times to meet the wish of one who had
that which he craved, found himself with a store of
what he did not need, while that which he wished was
possessed by another. The husbandman who began
business with a pyramid of huge grain baskets behind
him, found himself at eve, the possessor of a string of
shells, a few cotton garments or some pottery; while
the vendors of these now sat behind the baskets of grain
speculating upon their profits when they exchanged
with the strangers on the border.

When the hour of sunset came, the crowd thinned
and even the slaves rested; but as the big moon rose like
a great topaz, the people thronged the square, many of
them arrayed in new garments and decked with ornaments. The women eagerly displayed their latest ac-
quisitions to their friends, while the men had much to
say about new weapons, and implements, and the inci-
dents of trade.

"My eyes were filled," said one who wore the tunic
of a warrior, "with a certain breast piece of curious
workmanship which the stranger, Naqua, brought. It
has the property of turning aside the sharpest spear
thrust, and arrow points fall upon it like harmless hail.
I had nothing to exchange but a few pink shells, while
the men of the temple demanded two pieces of clear

turquoise, as large as a finger-joint, such as comes from the round hills beyond the desert. My heart ached with longing and the fear that some other breast than mine would bear the beautiful treasure. Who will desire my shells? Nevertheless I cried them among the merchants, and behold, one calls and asks view of them! He finds them of strange form, counterparts of certain others that he has tried to match for a present to his betrothed. But he had naught but baskets!

"I cried the baskets and found one whose careless slaves had ruined his so that the blue and yellow grains strewed the ground. To him I sold my baskets and traded the corn for a store of stone implements. I bore these to one who had turquoise from the round hills, and after much haggling received two clear pieces such as I required, and bore them in haste to the booth of the strangers. Despair seized me when I saw one holding my precious breast-piece while he offered its price!

"Such was the heat of my desire, that though he was my comrade, I disputed his claim so violently, that one of the yellow robes intervened, and, may the gods give him peace! he decided that I had the first claim, and my pieces being found superior to the others, the treasure was awarded me!"

"And I," observed another, "would delight my daughter with a green parrot, and for three hours I tried to convert two measures of large white onions

VIEWS IN SALT RIVER VALLEY, CASA GRANDE.

into a blue pearl!   Verily, the strangers will bear home great treasure!"

"Yet it has been said," remarked the first speaker, "that the Great Council has resolved upon the greybeard's adoption into the temple!"

"Such a thing has never been before, and I like not innovations!"

"Thou sayest! but he is a sage of great wisdom, at the end of life and desires rest in Mázacl.   It is said,too, that his people are akin to ours and dwelt with our fathers in the cities of the lakes.   He has already gained some knowledge of our mysteries, and a generation ago he saved the life of lord Huema!"

"May the gods keep evil from the land of Mázacl!"

*   *   *   *   *   *   *   *

The merchants generally mingled with the throngs in the square, but several kept close to their booths or piles of goods, not that there was any danger of theft, for this crime was severely punished, but those who preferred solitude were men who took pleasure in figuring up their profits.   Otherwise the market-place was deserted.

The lady Zaca, attended by a female slave, entered the market-place at the eastern end, walked briskly along the line of booths, looking, as she passed at the signs or totems of the merchants displayed in front of each.   She passed beyond the last and stood by a passage that led down to the floor of the amphitheater, used by those taking part in the games, and saw the white moonlight and the heavy shadows filling the pit. She paused a few moments stamping her feet upon the ground impatiently and then began to retrace her steps.

A booth built against a tree, on the very edge of the canal, which had escaped her observation, caused her to stop. Over a framework of sticks were thrown bison and bear skins and in front upon a pole was the gaunt head of a grey wolf. She saw the sign and uttered an exclamation, whereat the slave approached fearing that an insect had stung her, but she put her hand quickly to her neck and looking upon the ground, said she had lost a rare shell from her necklace, and bade the girl retrace the path they had come and search for it.

When she had left, the lady Zaca took an ear of corn from the folds of her garment and cast it into the booth, retiring into the shadow of a tree. Instantly a man came forth bearing the ear of corn, and standing in the light he broke it into three parts and waited. Then she showed herself, and he saw her and prostrated himself at her feet.

"Rise!" she said, "and speak quickly for time is precious. I received thy message by the slave. What tidings from the hills?"

"The people dream of thee and the fields of their fathers. The warriors are full of hope, and their valor chafes at inaction. A strange people from beyond the mountains have taught them to point their weapons with a metal that will pierce armor as the needle pierces the cloth."

"It is the red metal that we are forbidden to use!"

"Then it hath been changed by the gods, for it is neither red, white nor yellow, but something of all. It will cut the hard stone as the stone itself wounds the pulpy cactus. If it be the red metal of the gods, yet, as I say, it has been transformed. Have the gods not changed their minds in the past, and shall they not do it again? Shall not those who govern frame new laws and abrogate the old? Perchance they weary of the pride of Mázacl; weary of the priests who rule with a rod of iron, and throw sand in the eyes of the people! They will aid us to avenge our wrongs, employing us as the instruments of their wrath. Do the men of Yahvan control the gods! Will the lady Zaca, daughter of Tzah, the star of our hope, frown upon the counsel of the sages?"

"Thou art not slow of speech, Cazoc, and if thy arm be as ready as thy tongue, thou art a warrior fit to cope with Lionhead, himself!"

He smiled grimly and tossed his head.

"I listen," continued the lady Zaca, "to the words of the sages who, in the mountains are nearer the gods than the men of Yahvan hiding in the shadow of the walls of the temple. It may be true, as thou sayest, that the gods themselves have broken the bonds of custom in order that we may rest by the urns of our fathers. What hast thou further, and why temptest thou death by coming here?"

"We wait for thee as the darkened earth for the sun! When the sages that sit in the mouth of Ketecla asked: 'Who will bear tidings to the daughter of Tzah?' Cazoc answered, and he is here, and laughs at the men of Mázacl, whose pride fills their eyes with yellow humors, He will tell the sages that the daughter of Tzah has not forgotten her people; that she smiles upon them and bids them rest on their spears and have their bows strung with new sinews!"

"And thou wilt speak truly!"

Cazoc drew nearer to her and lifted the edge of her garment and pressed it to his lips. "Can the lady Zaca," he said, "hear that which is wild and impossible, and yet has such evidence of truth about it, that it may be believed—something that will stir her blood like new wine?—It is said that the lord Tzah perished not!"

She started and placed her hand upon her heart; then by a sign bade him proceed.

"It has been thought that he was killed in battle, but one has declared that instead, he was borne alive to the temple of Yahvan, and may still live there."

"Impossible!"

"So said the sages at first, and threatened him who told it with awful death, but he persisted in his story, and swore by his hoary head that it was true."

"How is it that he held back the story so long?"

"He fought with our fathers against the usurpers of Mázacl, and in the fray by the deep lake, received a blow upon the head that deranged his mind. He fled to the hills and lived upon roots and nuts for a generation. Then the gods restored him and he sought our people and told how he stood by the side of the lord Tzah and saw him overcome and borne off. He himself had been stricken down but noted all that passed. Thereafter a blow from the club robbed him of his mind, and when night came he probably escaped to the hills.

"Those who survived the fight remembered that the lord Tzah with many others, all of whom were accounted as slain, were separated from the rest, for when they pressed forward, the enemy appeared to give way; hence the story has much probability in it."

"I was an infant and hardly knew my father, but if he lives—no, it is not possible!—and yet he was of an age with lord Huema. The thought that I may have been living these years almost within reach of his voice, knowing it not, fills my soul!"

"There are those who believe that he still lives in a hidden recess of the temple, and Cazoc will discover if it be so or not, or die in the attempt!"

She placed a hand upon his sturdy shoulder, and

said: "I thank thee, Cazoc," while his blood thrilled with ecstacy.

Then he enquired about the strangers who had come from the far south, Naqua and Tzihn, and she told him that the former would be adopted into the temple and in time wear a yellow robe.

"I understand," remarked Cazoc, "that the people like it not that this honor should be conferred upon a stranger, and say that it will bring evil upon the land."

"The lord Huema loves him, and he rules Mázacl and the Great Council, which is, indeed, his servant; that makes the bondage seem to the people of their own making."

"And the other?"

She smoothed the ground with her sandaled foot before replying.

"He returns to his own people, but he is a great warrior, skilled in the use of all weapons, and I would fain have him remain and lend us his arms and be a brother to Cazoc."

A deep frown overspread the face of Cazoc, but the sound of footsteps distracted her attention so that she did not observe it.

"The slave returns! Be of good cheer, the gods are with us! Before next harvest time the flaming signal will rise in the air, a fiery messenger to the people who wait. Farewell!"

* * * * * * * *

The girl met her mistress less than twenty paces from where she had left her, and 'before she could speak, the lady Zaca told her that she had found what was lost, and chided her for staying so long!

CHAPTER VII

Take mystery from the world, and life appears
　A cheerless waste!　The dreams that fill
Our souls with fancies, hopes and fears—
Even our pains, and sorrow's bitter tears—
　Are better than Reality's dull chill!

AT sunrise on the third day of the feast, a rude alarum came from the summit of the temple, and the people hurried to the walls and along the canal. When the alarum ceased the face of the sun showed above the hills like a disk of gold, and the people shouted a welcome to the god of day.

From the great court of the temple issued a double file of men clad in red robes. Upon their heads were wreaths of green leaves and in their hands stalks of corn. Between two standards was borne aloft a square sheet of copper, polished so that it appeared to flame in the sunlight.

After them came others clad in black, bearing a disk of silver which looked like the queen of night when she shows her face behind thin clouds; and these were followed by a troop of maidens in white cotton tunics, their faces marked with blue lines, bearing flowers and green branches.

Then came a disk of gold, an arm's length in diameter, which flashed a greeting to the sun, whose emblem it was, and the people cried "Hail!" Those who followed the golden disk wore yellow robes and some bore baskets of ripe corn, seeds and nuts, whereof they cast handfuls into the air, and when they fell upon the ground, the people gathered them up and treasured them.

Following the escarpment, the procession made a full circuit of the temple, and reaching the point of departure, descended to the canal, and proceeded along its bank to the western end of the amphitheater, where it halted while the people took seats. Then it descended into the amphitheater and made three circuits, halting at the base of the pyramid facing the assembly.

A solemn hush fell upon the vast concourse as thirteen yellow robed men ascended to the apex of the pyramid, and there issued apparently from its bowels the sound of stringed instruments, like the sighing of the wind through stretched bowstrings, and the music followed their voices as they chanted the following:

> "Hail eye of heaven, gift of great Tzebu!
> Who on the White Wings crossed the wide waters!
> Out of the red stones, out of the gray stones,
> Man he created, woman he fashioned;
> Taught them all knowledge by the great water:
> Bade the earth serve them in seed-time and harvest;
> Commanded the sun-god to smile on the red earth:
> Commanded the seasons to come in rotation:
> Commanded the moon-god to lighten the darkness:

> Sprinkled with star-gems the deep vault of heaven.
> Taught he the mystical art of thought-writing,
> Spinning and weaving and earthenware making;
> All that is needful, all that man knoweth,
> Taught the great Tzebu, there by the salt sea!
> Finished his work—on the neck of the White Wings,
> Tzebu returned to the land where the sun sleeps!
> Left he the Skystone, the seal of his blessing,
> The eye of his soul and the seal of his promise!
> Left he the hope that our spirits will join him,
> In the land where the sun sleeps,
> At the end of the waters!"

The invisible accompaniment ceased with the voices, and while the people strained their ears to catch its last faint echoes, a great smoke shot with forks of flame arose from the pyramid and the singers prostrated themselves.

The smoke floated away like a great cloud, and behold, lord Huema stood where it had been and bore in his hands a small casket of ebony, and when the people saw it they bowed their heads, for it was the casket of the Skystone, the genius of Mázacl! Mothers drew their children closer, fearing its mysterious power, and strong men trembled, for it had come from the gods and had the power of life and death! And while the people still bowed, smoke and fire rose again from the pyramid and when it disappeared the lord Huema was no longer there!

The lady Zaca sat at the east end with the lord Lionhead and his family, and Tote sat below her by the side of Naqua. The lady Zaca marveled how the lord

Huema came and went with the smoke, but Tote held his head between his knees, and the sound of the strange music seemed to hum in his soul.

Naqua wondered why the Skystone had not been taken from the casket and shown to the people as it was a generation ago, and resolved to enquire the reason of lord Huema.

CHAPTER VIII

After the harvest, let the soul rejoice,
For labor is man's task and not his choice!
He needs, like plants, some sunshine with the showers
And suffers from the thorns, to win the flowers!

THE procession reformed and returned to the temple, and then the burden of fear was lifted from the souls of men, and their resilient minds returned to thoughts of pleasure.

The arena was quickly occupied by those who wished to take part in the Harvest Dance. Equal numbers of both sexes arranged themselves in sets of twelve, each set having a director. The dance began with a dreamy movement of the body and limbs, indicating the awakening of the forces of nature from the sleep of winter. The dancers shook their gourds, partially filled with pebbles, in harmony with their motions; the leaders squatting upon the ground, setting the pace by beating their drums and intoning a rough but rhythmic chant.

Then followed movements suggesting the irrigation of the land, its cultivation and seeding, and the dancers stooped and rolled their gourds upon the ground, rising again to their full height to indicate germination and growth. The ripening of the grain, the harvesting and garnering followed in their places, and at the end, the dancers circled in and out, set mingling with set around the arena. They embraced and struck each other's gourds, whirling in a wild frenzy of delight while they sang the Harvest Song:

"Sing to the red earth, sing to the sun!
Sing to the harvest—our labor is done!
Sing to the blue corn, the yellow and white!
Sing to great Tzebu, the father of light!
   Oo-ah-cha! Oo-ah-cha! Oo-ah-cha!
Sing to grey Winter, who soon will come forth
From his nest in the dark, cheerless caves of the north;
   On father the sun will come home from the south
And meet the white foam that he breathes from his mouth!
   Oo-ah-cha! Oo-ah-cha! Oo-ah-cha!"

After the dance came foot-races and ball-games, wrestling-matches and trials of skill with spear and arrow, those who excelled being rewarded with suitable presents and the acclamations of their friends.

The final, and most important event of the day, was a joust between renowned warriors. These to the number of twenty entered the arena, clad in blouses of leather and wearing caps of the same material which had visors that concealed and protected the face and bust. They were armed with blunt spears and bucklers of stout hide, and as they entered they raised their arms to the sun invoking a blessing.

Beyond the knowledge that all were worthy foes, for each had to submit to a certain test of skill before entering the lists, none was supposed to know his neighbor, and only the victor might reveal his identity. This arrangement left friend free to war against friend or brother against brother; no former prowess, no reputation for skill could daunt, and while it mitigated the bitterness of defeat and aroused no animosities, it excited the liveliest ambition.

Arranging themselves in line they made a circuit of the arena so that all might admire their muscular forms, and, as frequently happened, identify them by some peculiarity of walk or bearing, for the concealment of identity was often more theoretical than real. Having made the circuit they paired off indifferently, each exchanging weapons with his adversary. Then they fell to thrust and ward. The victory in each contest remained with him who first touched a vital part of his adversary's body with the point of his weapon, the marshals of the sports proclaiming the points and settling all disputes. The vanquished retired, bruised and crestfallen, amid the derisive shouts of the spectators, while the victor sought another, who, like himself had achieved success; and so on until one alone remained, and to him were accorded the honors of the day and a *corium* of richly chased leather made by the most skillful artificers of the temple.

The clash of spear and buckler, the rattle of wood and the dull thud of weapons that reached home; the wild plaudits of the crowd at some lucky stroke, and the cries of the marshals, grew fainter as the fight progressed and the general interest concentrated. When of all who had entered full of valorous ambition, one only remained, a solemn hush prevailed. His herculean frame showed no signs of fatigue, and his step was as springy as a young antelope's, as, according to custom, he strode around the amphitheater, striking his spear upon his buckler and challenging the world to dispute his supremacy.

Who was he?

Every one asked this question of his neighbor, and the answer was a negative shake of the head and shrug of the shoulders, for no one knew him. They knew, though, that the best spearsmen of the land had been vanquished, and there was none to dispute his claim to the prize of victory, save only the lord Lionhead, and he had won it so often in years gone by that he had modestly foresworn the joust. Nevertheless, all eyes turned to where he sat among the lords of Mázacl, a heavy frown wrinkling his brow and a strange light in his eye, as if to be assured that it was not he that stood in the arena like the god of war!

And as they gazed, behold, the victor came before the seat of the lord Lionhead and beat his buckler until it roared, and he cried to him derisively:

"Have all the lords of Mázacl won the right to sit with the women and children and have their slaves hold mats between them and the sun? Is there none among them willing to meet my spear and kiss the red earth?"

The people murmured loudly at this covert sneer, and the lady Zaca shuddered as she heard the voice, and her eyes closed in fear.

Tote raised his head and stared with amazement, but the lord Lionhead touched his shoulder and whispered in his ear; then with a smile he tied his long hair into a knot, threw aside his cloak of feather-work, and sprang into the arena!

When the favorite lord and warrior of Mázacl faced the vainglorious victor the people rose in their places and shouted and clapped their hands.

One of the marshals handed him a spear, but he refused a buckler in spite of the protests of those near him, and thus equipped, clad only in a loose garment, he exchanged weapons with his challenger, and the combat began.

Thrust succeeded thrust quicker than the eye could see, but the lord Lionhead wielded his spear so that it warded off the blows aimed at him, or by agile movements caused them to waste themselves in the air. He appeared to stand behind a palisade of wood, while the rapping upon his adversary's buckler showed that his weapon had a searching mind.

Breathlessly the people watched, and a great sigh of relief arose from laboring breasts, when the Unknown tripped upon the ground made slippery by his own

VIEWS IN SALT RIVER VALLEY, CASA GRANDE.

sweat, and exposed himself to a deadly thrust. But the lord Lionhead scorned to take advantage of an accident and stayed his hand until his adversary arose and recovered his defence, whereat there was great acclaim, mingled with low murmurs of discontent. In their excitement, the people descended into the arena to watch the contest, and the marshals were so absorbed that they were pushed forward and knew it not.

The contest was resumed with fresh vigor, the Unknown fighting with the ferocity of a wounded lion, and the other with the confidence of superior skill.

The garment of the lord Lionhead clung to his moist flesh and impeded his movements, and his long hair broke loose and fell about his neck and face, but he laughed at the eyes glinting at him like balls of fire through the holes in the visor, and shook back his locks like a young girl playing in the wind!

His spear looked like the shadow of a quivering bowstring, and his heaving chest showed its great muscles through the clinging garment, but his adversary, though he worked like a giant, exhibited no weakness.

The spectators began to think that neither could gain advantage over the other; but while they looked, two serpents seemed to spring forth, meet in the air and coil about each other; one of them flew twenty paces to the left and the Unknown fell upon his back with the point of Lionhead's spear at his breast!

A great shout rent the air, as the victorious lord bent by the head of the vanquished and said to him :

"I know thee, Cazoc the outlaw, or else I had not fought! The daring of thy malice betrayed thee! Thou wouldst dare the lion in his lair! Thou knowest thy life is forfeit by the act; but I give it thee in recompense for thy valor, so that thou tarriest not in Mázacl!"

CHAPTER IX

This world is real, and on substantial food
Our sensuous atoms feed, while, like a stream
Life flows between its banks of circumstance!
But when strange waters swell its burdened flood.
The narrow stream becomes a raging sea!

TOTE lay at the feet of Zaca by the pool, while the shadows painted the eastern walls and the doves cooed to the spirits of the night.

Her scarf of bright feather-work had fallen from across her bosom, soft as a pillow of *seiba* silk.

"Thou canst think of naught but the valor and skill of Lionhead."

"My lord is the son of a god!" cried Tote with fervor. "He has the strength of a bison, the eye of a panther, the lightness of a bird, and no man can stand before him! His spear is a darting serpent and multiplies itself so that it has the power of a score. It has life and reason in his hand!"

"But the Unknown did nobly, and had he not been worn out by many contests, it might have fared ill with thy lord!"

"Thou speakest like a woman, cousin! My lord had neither armor nor buckler, and exposed the nakedness

of his body to the point of the spear. He did but play
with his adversary until the sport wearied him!"

"Hast learnt his name?"

Tote hung his head, for he liked not falsehood, but
his lord's command was upon him, and he answered,
"No! He disappeared immediately ashamed of his own
temerity. If he were one that I could know, I fancy I
might prize his friendship, for he has a powerful thrust
and a keen eye!"

Zaca drew a long breath, for she had recognized
Cazoc and feared for him, if he should be known.

"I understand little of such matters indeed! I can
use the needle and the distaff, but the spear and buckler
I know not. To please thee, I'll view these things
through thine eyes, for I know that thou art true."

"Thou knowest!"

"Therefore I will ask a favor of thee!"

"Ask what thou wilt, and it is thine."

"Be not too rash in promises, for I may ask that
which thou canst not grant. Indeed, thou wilt refuse
me!"

"For thee, sweet cousin, I will stop a mad bison in
full career, or wrestle with a bear!"

"These are but feats of agility and strength. What I
will ask is more difficult, for he who fights with supernatural things, must have great sinews in his soul!"

"I do not comprehend!"

"And yet it is but to satisfy a woman's curiosity!

No, I will not require it of thee, and thou shalt serve me in some other way!"

The lady Zaca gathered his great locks of hair into her arms and combed them over her knees. She bent over them so that the pulsations of her heart sounded in his ear like the sweet music he had heard come from the pyramid. She reached to his forehead and smoothed back his hair and curled it over her arm. His heart nearly burst with delight and his soul sat upon the clouds!

"I love thee, Tote, and will not ask it of thee! I will ask, instead, that thou bringest me a fawn with eyes like thine own, to be my pet when thou art away with thy lord."

"Thou shalt have the fawn and all else thou desirest, and if thy heart were set upon the sacred Skystone itself, I would essay to get it!" and his eyes grew pink with ecstacy.

Without removing her arm, she laughed sweetly, and her voice sounded like that of the linnet when he sings to the morning star while the red rising sun paints his breast. The ripple of her laugh, and the perfume of her breath were fuel to his fervor.

"What I thought of asking thee, is neither so perilous nor so sacrilegious! Since nothing less will satisfy thee, I will tell thee what it is, and then thou wilt draw up under thy shell, like a frightened turtle!"

He held up his hands in protest, and she pushed him

back gently until he occupied his former position at her feet.

"Thou didst observe the mummery at the pyramid; the smoke and fire and how the hidden Skystone came and went! Some might think these things were supernatural, and that the lord Huema controls the spirits of the earth and air, but thou and I know that he is a mortal like ourselves. He moves upon his feet and casts a shadow in the light! Why should the Skystone be hidden in a box? Is it blind of age and long seeing? I have heard that it smiled upon our fathers at the great feasts, and are we less worthy to behold it? Didst thou not note that the lord Huema came and disappeared in fire and smoke as if he had been a spirit, while the awed multitude trembled like smitten slaves! The pyramid has a secret, and this is what I would know!"

Tote's face was marked with grey blotches while she spoke, and when she had finished, he said: "It is forbidden to ascend the pyramid, these six months!"

"Forbidden by the lord Huema, but not by the gods! What sanctity has been placed upon it? I can remember the time when the people sat upon it and good Popoche, when we were children, often took us to play upon it. Have not the decrees of lord Huema been disobeyed? Thou canst go there in the dark hour of the night unseen, and tell me what thou findest there, and if it be not a secret passage that leads to the temple, I am much mistaken."

She leaned over him as she spoke and played with his hair, and when her voice fell, he answered, "I will do it for thee!"

"When thou hast done it, I will look into thine eyes as thou tellest me, and thy heart will be glad because thou hast pleased me!"

*   *   *   *   *   *   *   *

Just before the rising of the moon, Tote tremblingly approached the base of the pyramid, and looked up at the dark mass, as if he expected it to belch forth fire and smoke.

His heart beat fast, and had he not seen among the stars the bright eyes of the lady Zaca, and felt her warm breath upon his face, he would have turned and fled. But these fancies animated him to the deed, and he ascended. Half-way up, he looked down upon the arena, and his imagination filled it with dark forms and rebuking eyes! He made no further pause, for hesitation unnerved him, and in a moment more he reached the top, gasping for breath, with the perspiration dripping from his brow. He saw nothing but a platform of large flat stones, and the simplicity of the matter vanquished his superstitious fears. He crawled along a few paces, to satisfy his curiosity, although he was confident that there was nothing extraordinary there, and certainly no secret passage to the temple!

He stopped and tried to cover with his view the unexplored area, and while his neck was craned beyond his body, the head and shoulders of a man shot up from the pavement, an arm's length distant! His surprise was so great that he could neither move nor speak for a few seconds.

His first impulse, when he recovered the use of his faculties, was to retire hurriedly before being recognized, but he reflected that the stranger had probably as little right there as himself, and if it were otherwise, the consequences of his own attempt to penetrate the secret of the pyramid were better met at once. His identity would certainly be discovered, for who could mistake his form! Then too he had promised Zaca to learn the secret, and it would be cowardly to fly the moment he was assured that there was one.

Before he was through with these ratiocinations, it struck him forcibly that the other party was following a similar course of reasoning, and that both were violators of the law, and equally criminal, and this impression was confirmed when the other asked in a low tone: "Who art thou, and what dost thou here?"

Tote was certain now that the individual was an intruder, and forgetting his own trespass, was indignant at that of the other.

Measuring the distance between them with his eye, he reached out his long arms, and before the stranger realized his intention, he was lying flat upon the platform, with Tote's great claws about his throat!

But he who had been fished up in such a startling

manner, proved to be a man of prodigious strength, and the fisher almost wished that he had not angled so well. The stranger struggled violently, and they rolled over each other several times, but before either asserted his supremacy, they fell into the pit, rolled down a flight of rude steps and came against a wall of wood!

The shock partially stunned them both, but Tote recovered first, and realizing that the confined space gave his adversary an advantage, he climbed back to the surface hurriedly. As one foot touched the platform, a hand from below seized the other, tripping him so that he fell upon his side with one arm under his body, and in a moment the stranger had him fast. The moon that had risen behind a thick cloud, peeped at the earth, and by its light, each saw the face of the other!

"Thou art Tote!"

"Thou art Cazoc, the outlaw!"

*　　*　　*　　*　　*　　*　　*　　*

"Thou rememberest me? Thou wast but a child when I fled to the mountains—a puny, misshapen toad—"

"Misshapen I may be, but puny thou hast not found me! Release thy hand and move thy mountain of conceit from my chest, and I will give thee such a tussle as thou never hadst before.

"Remember thee! I have seen thee since that time. Three harvests ago I saw thee by the skirts of the Twin Peaks, and thou didst fly towards them, thou and those with thee, as if your women waited thee with special longing! One of the warriors of Mázacl pointed thee out to me, and bade me mark thy well-shaped legs and heaving shoulders, as they worked to place thee beyond the reach of our arrows! I saw thee again at the tourney of warriors, but I looked in vain for thy shadow at the last, for thou didst lie upon it like a dead dog!"

This ironical reference to his defeat, made the blood of Cazoc surge in his veins like a flood rushing through a narrow gorge in the hills, but he closed his throat with a great gulp to keep back his anger, for he desired the good-will of Tote.

"Thou hast answered well, and proved that thy wit has the reach of thine arms; yet I spoke of thee as a child, and from childhood to man's estate is a long step! Now thou art Tote, the bison of Mázacl, and when thou shakest thy mane in anger, the pines on the mountains tremble, and the Tankmen hide their heads in the stagnant mud of their own pools! The grey wolf seeks the friendship of the bison, not his enmity!"

"Because the grey wolf fears for his shaggy skin!" added Tote with a sneer; nevertheless he was soothed by the flattery of the other, and before a reply could be made, he added in a milder tone: "If the grey wolf will remove his bony shanks from the bison's side, I will promise to do him no harm."

Cazoc desired no second encounter with the muscular hunchback, but he thought he would keep his word, and so released him.

Tote arose and shook himself and said: "Let us part in peace."

"Not yet," replied Cazoc, "for I have much to say to thee, before I go!"

"Then it must be said quickly and elsewhere, for here we cannot remain without risk of discovery. Let us descend."

Without another word, the suggestion was followed and Tote led the way to an obscure spot by the canal, where he seated himself upon the ground and waited for the other to speak.

"Thou art curious to know what took me to the pyramid?"

Tote nodded his head.

"I went to the amphitheater to look for something of value that fell from me when the lucky spear of Lionhead bore me to the earth. I was returning from a fruitless search when I saw some one approach the pyramid. I knew thee not, but was curious to learn what took thee there at such an hour, as well as being anxious for my own safety. I ascended to conceal myself and spy upon thee!"

The explanation was so plausible that his hearer saw no reason to doubt its truth.

"And now," continued Cazoc, "art thou willing to be as frank?"

"I went there, because the lady Zaca commanded me to do so!"

The outlaw was at first inclined to doubt the truth of this, but the statement came so artlessly, that he had to believe it, and it set him thinking.

The lady Zaca must have had some weighty reason for investigating the pyramid, a reason like his own, and in choosing her instrument must have confided to him some of her secret projects. The thought inspired him to speak with more freedom than he had intended.

"Thou knowest," he said, "that we are kindred, and though my love of liberty has made me an outcast and an enemy, we should remember this. It grieves me and others to see those who are of our blood, servants in Mázacl—servants to those who scourged our fathers and robbed them of their homes. If my voice has power with thee, it will move thy soul to detestation of thy dependent lot. It will inspire thee with a hot desire to share our freedom and our hopes. Our cause is that of the lady Zaca, and should be thine!"

"All that thou sayest," replied Tote in a low tone, "has been said before. It is like a dust cloud, that comes across the plain full of the promise of moisture, and fills our fields and houses with dirt. Why should I seek the liberty thou vauntest? What will it give me that I have not? Here I am at peace with those I love! If I followed thee to the mountains, the straight-limbed outcasts would see no kinship in my twisted body, and to them, as to thee, I would be a misshapen toad! Here the people know me and love me. My deformity has been seen so long, that custom has robbed it of ugliness, and only the strength it gives me is regarded. I seek no other liberty than the privilege of remaining as I am, and see no baseness in honorable contentment. I respect the urns of my fathers, but the dead have given me no command to war with the living, and my quarrels are my own. The ties of blood, thou speakest of, have been so far stretched that they are like the rivers that sink in the sand!"

"Yet, the sunken rivers rise again to refresh the thirsty land and gaze upon the sun!"

"What is once buried should stay buried, or else for what do people die?" answered Tote doggedly. "I shall stay with Lionhead and the lady Zaca!"

"What if the lady Zaca bids thee do this to serve her?"

He shivered as if struck with a chill. He hung down his head and gathered his knees into his long arms, and appeared to pay no further heed; but Cazoc bent over him and spoke fiercely into his ear:

"If I knew that I could trust thee, I could tell thee strange things! If thou lovest the lady Zaca thou wilt not betray me, for she is one of us. Thou, too, art one also, even though thou rollest thyself in the ashes; and thou canst not betray us without infamy. The men of Ilome who are outcasts in the hills, will wrest back their inheritance from the sullen priests of Mázacl. The greybeards have counted the stars, and the day of judgment is near; and when it comes the lady Zaca will be with us!"

Tote raised his head and in a voice hoarse with emotion, asked: "Does the lady Zaca know this?"

"Know it! she is the soul of our counsels, our evening and our morning star!"

The hunchback arose slowly, and clasping the trunk of a tree to steady himself, said: "I will not believe until I hear it from her own lips. Follow thou me!"

Leaving the canal, he led the way along the north side of the amphitheater and in the shadow of the temple by the embankment on the outer side of the encircling moat, until he came again to the canal in front of the dwelling of lord Lionhead.

Here he bade his companion wait, and crossing the bridge came quickly to Zaca's apartment. He scratched with his finger nails upon the mat of woven reeds that hung at the entrance and in a moment Zaca appeared. He told her hurriedly all that he had seen and heard, and demanded to know if Cazoc had spoken truth or falsehood.

Instead of answering, she bade him conduct her to the outcast.

When Cazoc saw her approach, he bowed his head to the ground, but she commanded him to rise and placed her hands against his shoulders and breathed upon his face!

And when Tote saw this, he held his hands over his eyes to hide the sight, as one places his hand upon the countenance of the dead, so that the memory of it shall not haunt him!*

---

*Ancient Gælic superstition.

CHAPTER X

Thought has its cycles, and the minds of men
Around the truth in different orbits roll;
And after circling in the vault of Time,
Through doubt and error, reach the self-same goal!

THE lord Naqua was adopted by the Great Council of Mázacl and accorded the highest privileges of citizenship, and though there were those who murmured, none openly condemned the act.

At his own request he was appointed a servant of the temple with the understanding that in due time he would be inducted to its holiest mysteries.

The gods were smiling upon him!

The wonderful Skystone was within his reach, and Tzihn, who would bear it back to his people, progressed rapidly towards recovery.

* * * * * * * *

The lord Huema showed him the different departments of the temple, excepting only the sacred chambers of the gods, which it was not yet lawful for him to enter. The present temple had been erected upon the ruins of one built by the people who came first from beyond the great river, before they knew that the land would be filled with their generations. It presented the appearance,

VIEWS IN SALT RIVER VALLEY, CASA GRANDE.

from a distance, of a single edifice, but was in reality, a conglomeration of many, built at different times. The original structure had been erected in the center, upon the summit of a mound formed of the debris of the ancient temple. Around this had been grouped a number of smaller buildings which were gradually united with the first, with occasional open courts for light and air. These had been elevated towards the middle, every addition and alteration being made so as to add to the symmetry as well as the convenience of the whole.

Upon the north side was the principal court where the people gathered upon occasions for religious exercises. Here, too, the products of the fields were received and measured before being stored in the granaries which occupied its two sides and extended some distance along the outer wall or row of buildings.

In the heart of the central cave were subterranean chambers wherein disobedient and criminal slaves were compelled to labor, finishing stone implements that had been roughly shaped by the hands of others.

They worked in darkness because the operation was so slow and tedious, that it disheartened the workman, and experience had shown that the hand was surer than the eye. The term of imprisonment being measured by the task, there was an incentive to faithful labor. This was the only art the slaves were permitted to learn, and the circumstances attending it were such as to make it abhorred. As no slave was permitted to enter the tem-

ple proper, these chambers were reached from without
by an underground passage that pierced the escarpment
on the north side below the court of the people.

The moat had evidently been formed, in the first
place, by the removal of the soil for the sun-dried bricks
and case-work used in the construction of the buildings,
and its utility as a means of defense afterward perceived, for while it completely encircled the temple, its
irregularity indicated the absence of original intention.

Most of the rooms on the ground floor were used as
store-rooms and public offices, and above them the artificers pursued their avocations. The skilled work-
men and their assistants were all free men, whose families resided without the walls. A fair compensation was
paid for their services, so that they were upon an equal
footing with their brethren of the fields. Weavers wove
the cotton into fabrics of different textures, and dyers
skilled in the preparation of pigments, colored them.
The dyes were fixed by means of a mordant brought
from the shores of the great sea; a kind of moss found
growing upon certain trees. The maguey and other
fibrous plants were prepared with considerable skill and
woven into cloth, coarse or fine, according to the quality of the filaments. The hair of beasts was worked
into warm cloaks and blankets for winter service, and
the richer materials were frequently decorated with
feather-work. The hides of the large animals were
tanned by means of a native root, rich in tannic acid,

and from the leather so obtained were manufactured, armor, saddles, moccasins and other useful articles, the artificers often decorating the material with rich chasings. There were workers of gems and shells, and engravers who reproduced the figures of men and animals with wonderful fidelity. The rushes that grew along the river bottoms were woven into mats, and baskets were made of the willow twigs.

Not the least important industry was pottery-working and in this the men of the temple excelled. The finest work was all finished by the priests who alone possessed the secret processes for coloring and glazing. Within the temple was a college for the education of the youth of both sexes, sons and daughters of the lords and warriors, and by this means, the priesthood held the minds of the people.

As a general rule, the children of the artificers and husbandmen were not admitted, it being deemed unnecessary for them to learn more than pertained to their industries. Nevertheless, every third son of these could be entered at the temple by permission of the Chief Keeper, as an incentive to the rearing of families. While this arrangement appeared to confine education to a class, it certainly added to its value, for what every one possesses is little esteemed. The admission of the third sons, opened the door of advancement to the humblest families, and since there was no law prohibiting intermarriages, the exclusiveness never appeared a hardship.

The real governing power was vested in the Chief Keeper, the Great Council being really an advisory body which met once each year, and did little else but approve his acts. While affecting to make rules for his guidance they followed his suggestions. They disturbed no established policy and originated no innovations. They asserted their independence by sealing all acts with their approval, and like wise legislators, pretended to do a great deal and showed their wisdom by doing nothing.

The people were pleased to be represented; the Council was proud to represent them; and the Chief Keeper was glad to be annually authorized to continue to please himself.

The Holy Chambers were in the heart of the pyramid and no one entered therein but the priests of the Yellow Disk. They were reached through winding passages, like a labyrinth, the way being known to the initiated only. Adjoining these were the apartments of those priests whose age and wisdom commended them as counselors to the Chief Keeper. His commands were made known through them, and with them he discussed the affairs of government, while to the younger and more active members of the fraternity was committed the execution of orders.

The lord Huema had two apartments adjacent to the

Holy Chambers, but not connected with them, and in the larger of these he received visitors. The other, adjoining it on the north, was of moderate dimensions used as a laboratory. It was entered from the first by a wooden door hung upon a central pivot and securely fastened by a secret contrivance of his own invention. Three of the priests only were able to open the door, these being specially chosen by lord Huema to share with him some of the higher mysteries.

*   *   *   *   *   *   *   *

During many days the lord Huema showed Naqua these things, and opened the eyes of his mind, so that they received the light of wisdom.

He brought from the inner chamber, two earthenware cylinders, sealed with wax, and opening them, drew forth several. rolls of yellow skin covered with brown marks, like thought symbols.

"These," he said, "are the chronicles of the friends and companions of Tzebu. More than a generation ago I found them among the treasures of the temple, and believed them to be the funeral urns of some holy sages of the past whose names had been forgotten like their ashes. I bade the lord Ataha, who has since found peace, place them in the Chamber of Death, giving them a most honorable place. He was old and of scant vision, and as he bore them over the threshold, he stumbled. The cylinder fell to the floor and came apart, exposing the rolls of skin. When he brought me the news, I knew that we had found the ancient records, that had not been seen for ages, for the art of preparing skin and writing thereon with black marks has been lost to us for many cycles.

"I found the characters dim with rage. They were strangely formed but not wholly unfamiliar, and I thought that with much study I might decipher them. For many years I devoted all my spare time to them, and light came to my mind and fear to my heart, for I learnt that which I dared not breathe to those about me —matters that shook the foundations of our faith!

"Thou, Naqua, hast traveled much; thy mind has broadened by contact with many races and creeds, and I can speak to thee as I cannot to my own people whose minds are narrowed by custom. I have indeed hinted of some of these things to those highest in my counsel, and might have gone further, had not the revolt of Ilome darkened my path. I am now impelled to make thee my confidant, as much for the reason I have stated as for the great need I have to unburden my soul."

"I am the most honored of the sons of men!" said Naqua, humbly, "and what thou sayest will be treasured in the sanctuary of my soul."

"O, Naqua, canst thou believe that the gods we worship are, like ourselves, ministers of an Omnipotence we cannot comprehend, or vain imaginations?"

"I have long thought it; yet, like a thirsty traveler, I keep the pebble in my mouth until I reach the water!"

"We deify the lights of heaven; the earth upon which we dwell; and they are brothers of the ants we crush beneath our feet! We personify the wind that blows upon our cheeks; the rolling thunder; the vivid lightning and all the phenomena of nature; and these are like ourselves, the servants of a power, revealed to our fathers and forgotten by their children. How it came about, I cannot guess, except that it is in the nature of man to throw aside the substance and preserve the shadow!

"Before I read these writings, I believed as others did. I bowed reverently before the gods of Mázacl and taught what I had learned, not so much because my heart was in it, as because I knew no other. Afterwards when the light came, I was bewildered, and daring not to do right did wrong with greater zeal. Deceiving men the more because I myself was undeceived! Thinkest thou, Naqua, that I shall be forgiven?"

"Shall the great power, thou speakest of, that holds up the vault of heaven, judge his creatures unrighteously? Shall He who holds the earth in his hand be blinded by its dust? Man falls like the tree, but the tree rises not again itself. Be comforted, for these are matters thou canst not control."

"I still permit the people to dwell in darkness and even maintain them therein."

"Canst thou make the blind see? You proclaim the rising of the sun from the summit of the temple, yet it would rise as quickly if you were silent. The people can see the sun and, therefore, they worship it willingly, but if you proclaim a truth invisible, will they not call you liars? It is no small matter to overturn the faith of generations, and reform is at first darkness:

"Thinkest thou that the people who have for ages worshipped sensible objects will turn at once to an unknown god whose attributes are so mysterious that thy reason cannot compass them? Will they believe those who proclaim themselves false prophets, even when they speak the truth?"

"No, lord Huema! Those who have led in error, shall not lead in truth, for the people will say, 'They seek to bind us with new ropes because the old are rotting!' The truth must come from without, and be arrayed against them who discovered it!"

"I understand thee, Naqua. Hereafter we will speak upon this matter again, and in the interval let it burden our souls!"

CHAPTER XI

A man and woman have two eyes alike,
But when they love, need but a single pair;
Then, what to one is beautiful and bright,
Is to the other, excellent and fair!

TZIHN lived in a world whose sun was the radiant form of Zaca! Her eyes were the evening and the morning stars; her lips the blush of dawn; her forehead the arch of heaven! Her breath was the air he breathed; her teeth the white gates of a temple, and when they parted for her voice, the gods spoke from their sanctuary, and the world was filled with melody! Her garments were soft and opalescent as the first leaves of the sycamore in the light of the rising sun; when they rustled in his ears, the world was full of freshness and beauty and his soul sang like the redbreasts in the mating season!

When he neither saw nor heard her, a dead moon wandered before the face of the sun, and yellow darkness covered the earth! She was the daughter of a god; the stars knew her and the clouds brightened when she gazed upon them, for the glory of her beauty was like a ray of light! His reverence ennobled his love, and he worshipped the passion that consumed him! He desired that he might remain as he was for ever, to be near her and live in the glory of her charms!

But his wounds were knitted, the congested muscles relaxed; his red blood bore nerve-building currents to every portion of his frame; and the spirit of youth called him forth into the glad sunlight!

*   *   *   *   *   *   *   *

The scarlet and orange of the frosted tree-tops were like the feathers of bright birds. The night-hawks circled in the air between the trees and sky, and a soft haze mingled with the blue smoke of the evening fires, empurpling the vistas between the trees. Across the clear firmament the dying light flushed in great waves of pink and gold that hung upon the hills like the glow of forest fires. From the summit of the temple came the salutation to the god of day that hung like a great ball of fire upon the pinnacles of the mountains; and the people paused to bow their heads to the west, and mutter a prayer for his return on the morrow.

But Zaca and Tzihn saw nothing but themselves. They were children prattling like a brook. When matter failed them, they filled the pause with fancies light as the fairy-grass that blows about the hills! He told of the land of his birth; of the many strange things he had seen and heard; and she drank in his words, with her face close up to his, like a hungry nestling.

"Far to the south," he said, "by the great turquoise sea, wherein the sun cools his hot face at eve, the people of Coyoa dwell. There the trees grow like rushes by the river; the torch pine, the cedar, the ebony, the rose-wood and the blood-tree. The flowers never cease to bloom and the air is drunk with fragrance. The feathery palm, zapote and guayava, the cacao and the plum grow in the valleys and the mountains kiss the skies! The parrot, and a thousand other birds of brilliant plumage fill the air with color and music.

"From the green savannah that fringes the coast, up a wall of rock by a path so steep that the unaccustomed head grows dizzy looking back, we reach the house of Tetza; thence the road is over a narrow causeway between two gulfs, at the bottoms of which whirl the swift waters of Tlaya and Tlapa, dark as the throat of night! At last we reach the red hills and the towers of the gods among the pines, and here is the land of Coyoa! Behind the Breasts of Coyoa that tower above the land, the dark mountains rise, tier upon tier, as if the gods had sought to build a stairway to the sky; and none shall pass and gaze upon the sleeping maiden, who knows not the secret paths.

"Upon the Breasts of Coyoa, the White Spirit rests forever; catching the souls of men as they fly upwards, and bearing them at night to the land of Kolatzl!

"Every day she sitteth above the dark pines, like a white crane on her nest! When she is angry because the souls of men come not fast, thunderbolts quiver in the air and lurid lightning flashes from steep to steep!

The earth trembles and the hills rock; the black clouds, the thick breath of Hahue, the god of storms, rush from the north, and a deluge falls upon the world.

"Trees fall like men in the front of battle and are borne like feathers on the rushing torrents; the big rocks roll hither and thither, bounding in the thick air, like rubber balls in the games, and the souls of men are loosed! Then the White Spirit is happy, and becomes as radiant as the bow of the rain-god.

"At night the White Spirit hides behind the Breasts of Coyoa, in the dark caverns of Yatzpol, for then the great cross flames in the southern sky, the cross of Azzu, who weeps for the sins of men. But he is pinned to the sky, like a trussed bird, by the arrows of Mazzai, the enemy of man, the father of Hahue. And the good Azzu shall stay there and never look upon the sun, until a man shall live through a long life and do no ill!"

"Being a god, has he no power to free himself and destroy the evil Mazzai?"

"He has; but he suffers that man may be redeemed and raised to the level of the gods, his first estate."

"I cannot understand why he should suffer, as thou sayest, and still have the power to end his own suffering and the reign of the evil one."

"Nor I, sweet lady! Yet, we must believe it, or be forever damned."

"If thou dost believe it, then will I also!" and she looked into his eyes as the fountains of her faith.

Tzihn's heart beat so wildly that he could not breathe, and his eyes lost themselves in hers.

But her vision went beyond him into another world, and when his sight returned again, her face was fair and cold as the moon's.

"Tell me," she said, "why you left your people—you and the lord Naqua!"

There was a note of command in her voice, but a sweet smile dimpled her chin, and a warm light suffused her eyes.

Tzihn knew not what to say, and while he hesitated, she read what was in his mind. She guessed that he would avoid the truth, and the thought pleased her, for the man who equivocates with prescient love becomes its bondsman!

"The lord Naqua might have been the first among the sages of Coyoa, for he excelled them all in wisdom, but he had traveled much, and the love of change was like a sickness with him. He loved to talk of all that he had seen, and there were many ready ears to listen. This did I and others; and our unrest so worked upon us that this expedition was planned. Like a maiden, too easily persuaded he drew back, pleading his ripe age and other circumstances; but still we pressed him, and at length he yielded and we came!"

"What thou hast said, O Tzihn, compares with what went before, as the rattle of a gourd to the deep voice of thunder! Thy words are like dry leaves! Thou blowest them about with thy breath and they rub against each other and make a whispering noise—but they are sapless! A man and a woman have each a pair of eyes; but when there is confidence and love, there is but one pair between them. They see all things alike, and what is fair to one, is bright to the other. There is neither strife nor concealment, for seeing with the same eyes, their thoughts are alike and the pearls of truth hang upon their lips like dew upon the flowers. It is plain that I am not thy dear friend, since thou dost withhold from me thy confidence, and usest thy tongue to ensnare my mind!"

She rose as she finished speaking and moved away; but he grasped a fold of her garment and stayed her. For a moment he forgot the language she had taught him and babbled away in his own tongue. While the words were meaningless to her, she understood his thoughts and, with a smile, resumed her seat.

He knelt beside her, full of penitence, and kissed her hand.

"There shall be but one pair of eyes between us, henceforth and they shall be thine! But first thou shalt promise me that what I say shall never pass thy lips, for I have sworn by the gods to tell it to no man!"

"But I am a woman, my Tzihn, and thou breakest not thy vow in telling me!"

CHAPTER XII

NAQUA had kept so close to the lord Huema, drinking words of wisdom, that beyond keeping himself daily informed of Tzihn's progress, he had neglected him.

He forgot that his susceptible countryman was exposed to the seductive influence of the marvelous charms of the lady Zaca, and when he remembered it, his conscience smote him. He had left him in the deep and dangerous water to sink or swim as the gods might will! Perhaps the witchery of her charms had already so completely ensnared his comrade, that the call of duty and honor would sound in his ears like a voice from the bottom of a well!

He excused himself to his teacher and lost no time in seeking Tzihn.

He found him sitting at his door staring at the sunlight and so deeply wrapt in his thoughts that he knew not Naqua was near until he felt a hand upon his shoulder, and saw his white beard. He started to his feet in confusion, and saluted him with a kiss,

"I. have been so engrossed in the mysteries of the temple, that I had almost forgotten thee, Tzihn! I pray thy forgiveness!"

Now Tzihn was not guiltless of similar neglect upon his own part and his conscience smote him and closed his lips.

"How fares it with thee, my son?"

"I am well, my father."

Naqua perceived that he referred more to the fullness of his heart and the joy of his soul than the condition of his body and knew that the poison of love was in his veins. Nevertheless, he deemed it wise to keep his thought to himself.

"It gives me joy," he said, "to know that thy health is restored, for the time approaches when thou wilt need it!"

The young warrior's face grew livid and his lips froze together.

"Every fourteenth day," continued Naqua, "is a day of rest in Mázacl, when no man shall labor. Upon that day the priests enter the Holy Chamber and pray for the souls of men. To-morrow is the beginning of a new week, and the day following the second day of rest thereafter is the intercalary day of the Mázacl year, which has thirteen moon months. Upon this day I shall be invested with the yellow robe and be free to enter the Holy Chamber. After that I shall be dead to the law of my fathers, but though dead my hands shall send them a blessing."

A deep sigh swelled in his chest and rattled in his throat. His eyes grew dim with tears and his grey head hung upon his breast like the flower of the ripe corn.

Tzihn was moved with compassion. He stretched out his arms and beseeched him to go no further in his act of sacrifice.

Naqua mastered his emotion and raising his eyes to heaven said: "It is too late, even if I would. I have come to the brink of the dark river and Azzu bids me cross! Shall the warrior, full of the vigor of manhood, with the joy of new-crowned love in his breast, offer his bright life in the front of battle, and I, a blasted pine upon the hill-side, solitary and sapless—I, to whom the joys of life are stale and tasteless—refuse the sacrifice of this tottering life? No, by Azzu the redeemer of men! It is for thee to do thy part, and I will do mine!"

Tzihn knew then that so far as Naqua was concerned, his fate was determined, and his heart sank.

"About the time of which I speak, I will ask permission for thee to return, pleading thy great desire to breathe thy native air and kiss the cheeks of thy kindred and friends and enrich them with the products of our trafficking. Thou shalt bear with thee that which is more precious than all other gems—the Skystone which we came for; whereby the curse shall be stayed from our people! The White Spirit shall cease to haunt the

Breasts of Coyoa and generations shall bless us. With
half a score of suns to start thee on thy way, it will be
strange if thou out-journeyest not those that may follow thee."

"And thou, father?"

"Think not of me! If the loss is charged against me,
I shall die, and in doing this I do no more than did our
brothers by the river."

"Thou movest, my father, like a storm cloud bearing
bane and blessing, but with a rush that affrights, so
that the first only is seen. Thou hast been filling thy
mind with wisdom while I have been like a caged bird.
My muscles are like the soft sinews of a new-killed deer
and my lungs hold not my breath! I know nothing of
this land or its people, and when I return I shall be
dumb respecting its wonders!"

"There is some reason in what thou sayest, but a
greater still moves us to haste. My conscience gnaws
at my soul like a hungry wolf when I think how the
lord Huema loves and trusts me. Each day increases
my sense of gratitude and weakens my resolution to be
ungrateful. If thou lovest me; if thou lovest the land
of thy birth and the people of thy blood thou wilt goad
me to the deed from which I shrink. Like Azzu I am
nailed to the cross for the sins of men!"

His head fell upon his breast and his frame shook
with the violence of his emotion.

Then the heart of Tzihn melted and he swore to himself that he would emulate this great self-sacrifice and deny his love!

"Yet, indeed, thou shalt see the land," continued Naqua when he found his voice again; "for it is well for thee to do so. Thou shalt go forth into the hills and hunt the horned sheep and the bear, for thus thou shalt prepare thy limbs for the long journey before thee. Tote will go with thee and a band of warriors, although there is no danger, for during the thirteenth month there is peace with the outcasts. When thou returnest, I will be ready!"

After discussing some details, he returned to the temple, and when he was gone Tzihn turned and beheld the lady Zaca standing like a white spirit upon the threshold.

"I have heard all," she said, "and the lord Naqua is wise in bidding thee go to the hills to strengthen thy weak limbs!"

"Thou, too, art anxious to see me go?"

"I said thou shouldst go to the hills!"

"But thou meanest—"

"What I say! But thou shalt not return as Naqua desires!"

"I comprehend thee not."

"Thou art dull to-night. To-morrow thy wit will be sharper; then I will speak more plainly!"

"Can I be a traitor to Naqua and my people? Shall I forswear duty and honor—"

"If thou lovest me, thou hast given them in keeping to me! Thy life is my life; thy thought is my thought; and being true to me, thou art true to thyself!

"I will hold thy head in my arms! Thou shalt look into my eyes and read thy thoughts there! Then thou shalt choose between thy people and Zaca and hers!"

* * *

And he said: "I choose thee and thine!"

CHAPTER XIII

Out on the *mesa,* where the tawny plain
Bends to the purple hills and pearly sky:
Where the air shimmers like a sun-kissed sea,
And Nature lolls in dreamy ecstacy!

TZIHN and Tote, with a small band of warriors, camped the first night between the two rivers that water the valleys of Mázael and Ilome, on the western edge of the plain by the Hills of the Giants, Katzut.

The land was like a great park, with trees of mesquite and iron-wood over a carpet of long grass.

While the slaves who bore the water gourds and provisions were preparing supper, Tote recounted the legend of Katzut.

*   *   *   *   *   *   *   *

"In the days when the gods walked the earth, they had habitations upon this plain and here they rested unmolested by the petitions of men. The plain then stretched from river to river and was covered with tall trees, that now grow only in the mountains, and beautiful flowers. The sweetest singing birds in the world sang in the branches of the trees and the wild beasts roamed through the forests without enmity to one another. There came from the north a race of giants, sons of Mazzai. When they saw the gods living like mortals they despised them and challenged them to combat for the dominion of the world.

"The gods laughed at their impudence, but the giants were vain of their great strength and stature and said: 'Who can withstand us!'

"They stepped across the river and trod down the trees and the flowers. The birds flew to the south and the beasts sought refuge in the mountains. They cast great stones upon the plain to crush the gods and their houses. On the edge of the plain and as thou goest westward to Coyal are the stones they cast, like great hills.

"Then the gods were wroth and sent the spirits of the air to blow dirt into their faces; but the giants spat against the dirt and it became mud under their feet. Seeing this the gods awoke the Earth-god, who was sleeping. When he saw the giants and how they disfigured the plain he shook with anger so that the mountains toppled over. He opened his great jaws and swallowed them as if they had been so many ants.

"In his stomach they became great rocks which he cast up and they are the hills of Katzut which thou seest. No man shall set foot upon them and live, for the souls of the giants are imprisoned in the rocks. In the pass, facing the Bear's Head, thou shalt see some of the giants standing erect, as in life, a thousand arms in height!"

* * * * * * * *

Tzihn feared not as he looked upward at the great cliffs kissing the darkening sky, and the columns of rock frowning upon the valley; for the lady Zace had told him that there Cazoc would meet him and lead him to the sages that sat in the mouth of Katecla!

* * * * * * * *

At dawn, Tote awoke the son of Coyoa, and pointing to the southern edge of the horizon, cried: "Behold the habitations of the gods!"

Tzihn turned and saw a lake of crystal water, whereon were mirrored the sky and the clustering trees upon its shores.

Amid the verdure, grey towers and purple pyramids caught the blush of dawn, and temples rose from the bosom of the lake. As he gazed, the scene was changed like a dream, until it disappeared, leaving the plain and the purple hills hanging upon its edges.

"It is an illusion!" he said.

"Call it what you will," observed Tote. "I know that it is the home of the gods that we have seen, and no man shall reach it in life! Can the eye see things that are not?"

* * * * * * * *

They turned slightly to the north and entered the opening between the hills through which they could reach the mountains beyond; and the giants of stone seemed to move down the hillside to meet them. The warriors muttered short prayers to the gods and drew closer together.

As the sun rose well above the hills, a dark cloud shaped like the head of a bison appeared in the south. It rolled towards the east, with a long tail like a serpent's and looked as if it would break over the valley of Ilome.

"It is lucky that it comes not our way!" remarked one of the men; but even as he spoke it ascended like a whirlwind, twisting and turning and lashing itself in fury. Half way of the zenith it broke into the shape of a bow bending against the mountains of Katzut!

"The storm-god has seen us!" cried Tote. "We must lose no time in reaching higher ground, or we shall be overwhelmed!"

Forked lightning leaped from the center of the storm and zig-zagged across the plain, while the cracking thunder echoed in the hills. Before them at the distance of about a mile was a piece of rising ground and the party moved with all haste towards it, for the soil under their feet was soft and broken. A herd of antelope rushed by them, seeking a place of safety, their instinct warning them of their danger. From a smart walk, they broke into a trot, and when they heard the rushing water at their backs and felt the fierce air pressed forward by the storm, they dropped their more cumbersome burdens, and ran swiftly.

Before they reached the hill, the cloudburst fell upon them! There was no air to breathe; the soft ground turned to mud and held their feet, and the water rose about them like a deluge! Blinded, breathless and bemired, they turned their backs to the storm and waited for it to pass! It swept by them to the hills, in a few moments, but the water gathered where they stood, fed by rushing torrents from the plain. They had no time to lose!

They struggled forward like drunken men, pitching and stumbling, and saw the place of safety not fifty paces away.

But the hope that rose in their hearts was choked in an instant, for the storm after touching the cliffs of Katzut returned over its path with redoubled fury as if the frozen giants had breathed their hate into it. With a wild cry of alarm, they cast aside all that encumbered them and when the fearful tempest struck them in the face, the hindmost were swept away like dry leaves!

*   *   *   *   *   *   *   *

Tote and half a dozen others reached the firm ground by a miracle, and when the storm passed, they saw that Tzihn was not among them! It was more than an hour before it was safe for them to leave their place of refuge, and during that time the hunchback suffered the acutest mental anguish.

Not only did he like Tzihn, but the lady Zaca had charged him to see that no harm befell him.

"She will curse me now, for bringing sorrow into her life! Why should the gods take the straight-limbed and beautiful and leave the deformed and ugly?"

He indulged in this mood until it became possible to descend to the lower ground; then he determined to explore the country in the hope that by some accident, Tzihn and other members of the party had escaped. The possibilities were entirely against it, he knew; for no living thing could have withstood the rush of waters.

Nevertheless he and the other survivors plunged into the mire as a matter of duty, for hope there was none. The ground was cut up into ravines and gulches as if it had been plowed and furrowed. They turned over the masses of slimy debris that might conceal a body, and followed the fissures down to the valley which opened out into a great rock-strewn wash. They searched the higher ground, ascended every hillock, examined every tree and bush, but found not so much as a sign of the victims! The day was nearly spent when they returned to the scene of the catastrophe, and took counsel.

Tote was anxious to remain and continue the search on the morrow, but to this the others refused to consent. They were without food since morning and spent with toil, and another day would undo them. It was wise to rest a couple of hours and return to the settlement, and then after recuperating and obtaining supplies they could return!

Tote yielded ungraciously, and towards dawn of the

following day they reached a village upon the main canal, and sent a messenger thence to tell the story in Yahvan.

*   *   *   *   *   *   *   *

When Zaca heard it, a dull ache came to her heart. She hid herself in her chamber and neither ate nor spoke for three days and when she came forth her face was pinched and wan and her eyes marked with great black rings under them.

A few days thereafter, lord Huema noted with alarm that Naqua had diminished in stature as much as a finger length; that his breath rattled in his throat, and his voice choked when he spoke!

CHAPTER XIV,

Till the last gasp there's hope!
  For who can measure out the sands of life?
  Out of the womb of Death, salvation comes—
    And Peace, herself, is born of blood-stained Strife!

But a miracle had happened—for Tzihn lived!

When the returning tempest came against them like the breast of a great wave, wiping out their view of heaven and earth and deafening them with its roar, he bent before it and held his breath. He clutched a thorny shrub, but it gave way in an instant, and he rolled like a rubber ball before the seething water. He struggled with feet and hands to stop his wild career, and thought his time had come.

When the cloud passed he found himself in the middle of a torrential stream with boulders and upturned trees, that threatened death. As one sees objects in the brief instant of a lightning flash, he beheld at the distance of a dozen arms' lengths, a stout tree over-reaching the torrent, and one of its branches swayed in the water! With a faint hope in his heart he raised his hands. At the same moment a floating tree came against him and lifted him up against the branch which he grasped with the desperation of despair! The force of the torrent was such that his added weight brought it beneath the water so that the character of the peril was changed only. He knew that the water would soon run by and if he could endure for ten minutes—aye, even five, he might be saved! But he was spent with bruises and labor; the current pulled him with the force of ten men; the stones and trees pounded him as they passed and he felt his hold weakening! He closed his eyes and breathed a prayer to the gods!

Strange to say, no thought of Zaca came to him; but he saw the White Spirit come down the mountain side by the Breasts of Coyoa, and her face was black as night!

She reached out great arms like twisting serpents to seize his soul and he felt himself pulled upward by the hair of his head! The water appeared to fall from him and its roar slumbered in his ears! He opened his eyes expecting to see Death, and found himself hanging across the limb of a tree with his feet dangling in the water and his head upraised against the knee of a man who sat astride a higher branch.

His savior by a gesture urged him to ascend still higher.

The instinct of self-preservation gave him strength and energy and in a little while he sat by the side of his preserver, faint from exhaustion. The roar of the torrent made speech useless, and the two looked at each other.

The light of gratitude shone in Tzihn's eyes, but those of the other were downcast and sullen as if he had done a good deed against his will. When the water had subsided, the son of Coyoa took the stranger's hand and held it against his own heart and said in the language of Mázacl: "I thank thee!"

The other smiled grimly and for answer signed him to descend.

Tzihn did so with great difficulty and when he tried to walk he fell forward, for every joint in his body appeared to be dislocated.

Perceiving this, his preserver took him upon his broad back and bore him with comparative ease to a gravelly knoll where he rested a few moments, and while he rested he spoke no word, but sniffed the air like an enraged bear.

Tzihn again essayed to walk, but failed, and was borne as before up the side of a hill into the midst of a pile of great rocks.

Here the stranger dropped him, like a burden, upon the ground, and disappeared. He returned in a few moments with a small gourd and a bear skin. From the gourd he gave him a draught of a fiery liquor which burnt his throat and tingled in his blood. Then he stooped down and offered to remove the girdle about his waist.

This action brought to Tzihn's mind certain tablets the lady Zaca had given him for the sages in the mountains and which he had placed in a leather pouch for better security and convenience in carrying. He put his hand to his waist and his joy was great when he found it still there.

When the other saw that he would not be permitted to remove the girdle, he gave a low grunt of displeasure and tossed Tzihn the bear skin and walked away.

When he was gone Tzihn drew the skin over him, and in a few moments the liquor he had drank sent him to sleep.

When he awoke, the stars were twinkling and the air was sharp. With a slight effort, he rose to his feet and found that he could walk with comparative ease.

Where was his rescuer?

Lifting his eyes he saw his form silhouetted against the sky upon the summit of a rock, and he went towards him. When the other saw him, he descended and spoke to him in the language of Mázacl.

"Thou art he who should come from the lady Zaca to meet Cazoc?"

"I am he—and thou art Cazoc!"

"I am the grey wolf of the mountains whom the drones of the plains call Cazoc the Outcast! I saw the men of Mázacl enter the pass of the giants and guessed that thou wert with them. The sky fell and I sought refuge in a tree. The gods sent thee to me and I have brought thee hither—for what may befall thee!"

There was a sinister tone in his voice that troubled

Tzihn, but he could not think ill of one who had not only saved his life but borne him to safety and cared for him like a brother. Nevertheless, he asked him why he had not made himself known before.

Cazoc gave a grunt and said: "I needed my breath for other purposes! Thou art no feather-weight to carry through the mire and up hill!"

"Were any of those that came with me saved?"

"That I know not, but the chances are that they lie buried in the sand and mud, beaten to death by the great stones or drowned in the waters. Their urns are not made by hands and their women shall not mingle burnt hair with their ashes for none shall find them!"

Tzihn covered his face with his hands and sighed.

"Thou hast fasted long," observed Cazoc, "and must be hungry!"

Tzihn acknowledged that he was and he followed his companion behind a large tilted rock under which was a cave of moderate size. Cazoc produced a gourd of water, some toasted deer flesh, parched corn and seed-bread and they seated themselves and ate.

When they had finished, they stretched themselves upon the ground, covering themselves with warm skins, and slept.

*   *   *   *   *   *   *   *

Tzihn awoke in the morning twilight and saw Cazoc bending over him.

"We must be going!" said the outcast.

They ate of the food left over from their supper, after which Cazoc bundled up the skins and hid them in a crevice of the rock.

When all was ready for their departure, he opened his lips for the first time that morning to ask Tzihn if he had any message from the lady Zaca.

Tzihn pointed to the pouch at his girdle and replied that he had a package of tablets to be delivered to the sages.

A strange light sparkled in the eyes of the outlaw; but he turned away so that Tzihn saw it not. They went further and stood upon the brow of the hill, above the Bear's Head, and looked across the plains towards Yahvan; and the plain was covered with mist upon which iridescent colors played as if a rainbow slept upon its surface. They followed the high land to the north through a rugged country where the rocks rose like the teeth of a comb, till they reached the edge of a gulch that appeared to descend into the bowels of the earth.

To the right of their path a shelving rock hung over the dark chasm, and Cazoc climbed up the rock, his companion following him. The surface was large enough to hold twenty warriors and it trembled in the wind that swept through the gulch. It was covered with large stones marked with signs, and carefully arranged in lines radiating from a common center. After

Cazoc had examined them carefully he removed one to
a different position and descended.

Tzihn's curiosity was aroused and when they came
together in the path he inquired what the stones meant.

"It is a house of signs," answered Cazoc, "whereby
our people can be informed of the movements of
others!"

They reached the bottom of the gulch with much difficulty and followed it upon a descending grade until
they came to the bank of a river where they encountered
a large company of men bearing baskets of grain and
seed.

"These," said Cazoc, "are men of the hills who come
from the boundary of Mázacl with the products of their
traffic, for on the thirteenth month there is peace between us, and it is unlawful to kill," and his eyes
gleamed with fury as the last words came with a hissing
sound. They ate with the traffickers and afterwards
crossed the river, entering the heart of the mountains
that lay beyond it.

Towards nightfall they approached a place where
great cliffs came together and their way appeared to be
stopped; but as they neared the walls of rock, a passage
opened and they saw a valley beyond encompassed by
towering pinnacles reddened by the sunlight so that they
were like great banks of flowers. Their path was cut
out of the face of the cliff and looked like a brown
thread as it rose before them and it reminded Tzihn of

that which led up from the savannah of his own land to the home of Tetza; but there was no blue sea kissing the sky behind him, only the black hills! The ascent ceased when they came to a point of rocks one-third of the way up the cliff, and while they paused for breath Tzihn's eyes opened wide with wonder at what he saw.

The valley was a vast amphitheater enclosed by shaggy cliffs and peaks of grotesque and awful shapes. One had the semblance of a human head as perfect in outline and feature as if fashioned by the hand of a sculptor. It rose gradually from a debris of rocks dwarfing all the other marvels of the scenery and appeared endowed with life as the changing light gave expression to the face. Above it hung a low cloud of thin smoke like grey hair and in its mouth were pillars that looked like teeth!

Cazoc observed the wonder and dread of Tzihn and said mockingly: "Fear not the giant's head until thou art between its teeth!"

And while they sat and rested, he told him the legend of Ketecla.

*   *   *   *   *   *   *   *

"He was of the race of giants whom the gods destroyed before they made men. When the great Deluge came upon the earth, they wished to spare Ketecla for he was descended from a god. They commanded him to ascend a high mountain and close his eyes so that his heart would not shrink at the destruction of the earth or his arm reach out to save his kindred. But Ketecla believed not that the gods could bring enough water to drown the earth, and the bad blood that was in him, caused him to mock at them. Nevertheless he ascended half way up the mountain, and then laughed so loud that it shook the water from the sky and the torrents filled the valleys so that he had to move up higher. This so enraged him that he climbed to the top and reaching at the sky, gathered a handful of dead moons and cast them into the waters.

"But though the moons were burnt out they were hot and dried up the water when they fell; and when there was no water they burnt the earth about the mountains whereon the giant stood. He stormed and cursed and sought water to extinguish them with. But the sky and the earth were both dry and the moons grew hotter and hotter. They melted the earth so that the mountain fell, and Ketecla sank with it into the pit of fire!

"Then the gods brought water from the great sea and filled the pit, and a great steam rose to the sky and remade the clouds that Ketecla had destroyed and the Deluge came. When the waters returned from the earth, the head of Ketecla remained above the pit as thou seest it now, for being one of the gods he could not be utterly destroyed.

"The grey cloud thou seest above his head is the breath that comes through his nostrils from the great fire that burns forever in his bowels!"

*   *   *   *   *   *   *   *

When Cazoc had finished they arose and entered the valley and came to the houses built against the cliffs under the toothed jaws of the giant!

CHAPTER XV.

TZIHN slept well for he was weary, and when he awoke he knew that it must be late although the chamber in which he had been lodged was dark. He remembered that Cazoc had brought him well into the valley, and after they had eaten a frugal supper he had taken him up a ladder placed against the cliff. A subdued light entered the chamber from one direction and he saw that he was in a large cavern.

He arose to explore his surroundings and advanced along a narrow passage through which the light came, and entered another chamber which opened out upon the world of sunshine. Through a narrow opening he saw the tops of trees and the white light glinting on the rocks. As he moved towards it, a man rose from below bearing a vessel of water and some food, which he offered to Tzihn. The young warrior was hungry as a wolf and forgot to be curious in the satisfaction of his appetite.

When he had finished he asked many questions, but

the man gathered up the empty vessels and disappeared by the way he had come without making reply. This conduct puzzled Tzihn and he was about to follow him down the ladder when he heard footsteps behind him and turning around, beheld two men armed with stout javelins and clubs.

"The sages," said one, "await the stranger to receive the message that he bears from the plains!"

"I am ready," was the reply, "and will follow you!"

"The path is dangerous to unaccustomed eyes, and for thine own safety we must blindfold thee!"

"I am used to scaling mountain cliffs where the eagle builds her nest!"

"Nevertheless it has been so commanded by the lord Tacantla, and it must be done!"

Tzihn was disposed to resent this as an imputation upon his courage, and inquired sharply for Cazoc.

"He has been called hence," was the reply, "but left word for thee to obey the lord Tacantla in all things for the sake of thy message!"

He then thought it prudent to submit, whereupon the men placed a bandage over his eyes and led him, as he thought, into the bowels of the earth, until they came to a place where he felt a great heat and heard a noise like the rush of wind through a narrow opening. Thence they ascended a hundred steps hewn out of the rock, and as they neared the summit, voices were heard and the bracing mountain air filled their lungs. At the top of the steps they halted, and one went forward to give notice of their approach and returning presently, the three advanced until Tzihn felt a sensation of light and knew that he was in the presence of the sun.

His guides removed the bandage from his eyes and in a few moments he saw that he was in a large chamber in the cliff for he saw the valley beneath him between the pillars of stone that stood in the opening.

In front of him with their backs to the light were a score of venerable men seated upon mats, and he took them to be the outcast sages of Ilome, the friends and kindred of Zaca.

He bowed his head and said: "Peace be with you!" and one answered: "As it shall be!" but the rest were mute.

One of his guides spread a mat at his feet and he sat down and surveyed the assembly, waiting to be questioned.

From a dark corner of the chamber there came an old woman, with glittering eyes, mumbling words that had no sense. She looked into his face, patted him on the back and squatted beside him. He moved away a little, but she followed him, and as no one else appeared to regard her, he imitated them and ceased to mind her.

"Thou comest from Mázacl with a message from the lady Zaca, whom the gods preserve!"

The speaker sat in the front of the greybeards and

spoke as one in authority, and Tzihn judged that it was the lord Tacantla who addressed him.

"Thou hast said, lord!"

At the sound of Zaca's name the old woman rose to her feet, and swaying her body to and fro, chanted rather than spoke:

"Where is the child of my bosom, the daughter of Tzah! Sweeter than the honey of the hills and the juices of the flowers! Whose lips are like the red berries of the mountains; whose cheeks are like the white mist of the morning; whose eyes are brighter than the evening star; whose breath is as fragrant as the lily of the valley! Cursed be he who lured me from her side to place my dry hand on the face of the dead!

"Where is Zaca, my beloved? Her voice sings in my ear and her soul mingles with my soul and yet I see her not! Where is she, the pearl of Ilome, to whom I taught the secrets of life-giving which the mother Atue won from Tanach the physician of the gods! The spirits of herbs and trees, the oil of vipers and the dew of the stars! Lost to Popoche—lost! lost!"

Her voice ended in a wail as she resumed her seat and hid her face upon her knees.

When the old woman, Popoche, was silent, the lord Tacantla spoke again:

"Who and what art thou?"

"Tzihn, of the people of Coyoa, who dwell by the

turquoise sea under the cross of Azzu who shall redeem the sons of men."

"Thou speakest as if thy people were our equals; yet we know that the gods have made none like us!"

"The people of Coyoa came like yourselves from the Cities of the Lakes and their father was Tzebu, the light of the world!"

The sages conversed in low tones, evidently discussing this matter, and Tzihn surmised that they doubted the truth of his statement; whereat he was angry, but the lord Tacantla spoke again before he could utter the words upon his lips.

"Thou bringest a message from the lady Zaca?"

"It is here!" he said, and he unloosened the pouch from his girdle and handed it to the speaker who rose to receive it; and when he had taken it, he held it against his forehead for a moment.

"Thou wilt find therein," continued Tzihn, "the tablets given me by the lady Zaca to be delivered to the sages that sit in the mouth of Katecla."

"Knowest thou what she wrote thereon?"

"This I know: that she commended me to the sages as a faithful friend devoted to her service, and bade me counsel with them as to how I could best serve her!"

Lord Tacantla opened the pouch and shook the contents out into his hand, and behold, instead of the tablets, there fell a few pebbles!

Tzihn sprang to his feet, quivering with rage and

protested that some villain had stolen the tablets while he slept.

His protestations were received with sullen silence and the men with javelins and clubs came closer to him.

His thoughts flew wildly from Cazoc to Tote and back from Tote to Cazoc—surely one or the other was guilty!

Both had acted strangely, yet they were equally sworn friends of Zaca and knew that he was under her protection!

The moody looks of those about him could not awe him into silence and he raved wildly, calling upon the gods to bear witness to his honesty.

But his words were like the ocean beating against granite rocks; they came back upon his soul and crushed it with nameless terror.

"Talk not to us, vile stranger, of thieves!" said lord Tacantla with an ominous frown. "We know the truth from Cazoc!"

This name appeared to excite Popoche to frenzy for she bounded to her feet and tore at her hair.

"Cursed be the grey wolf that rends the white limbs of children! May Mazzai catch his soul when he dieth the unknown death!" and with a maniacal laugh she fled from the chamber.

It was Cazoc then who had stolen the tablets! and

Tzihn dug his nails into the mat upon which he sat and tore it in his rage.

"From the noble Cazoc we have learned," continued Tacantla, "that thou hast dared to lift thine eyes to the daughter of Tzah, and she sent thee hither to be judged according to our laws!"

Tzihn half rose to his feet to speak, but was forced back at the point of a javelin and commanded to be silent at the peril of his life.

"But this is not the greatest of thy crimes! What brought thee to the land of Mázacl? Was it not to steal the Skystone—the heritage of Ilome and the crown of Tzah, the successor of Tzebu? Answer if thou darest!"

Tzihn stared at him with glassy eyes, looking through the meshes of the web that fate had thrown about him, and answered not, for he could not deny his guilt.

"Thy silence condemns thee! Helped by the gods of her fathers, who sleep not, the lady Zaca penetrated thy designs and sent thee to judgment!"

Temporary madness came to Tzihn and with a cry, like a wounded panther, he sprang upon the lord Tacantla.

He clutched him by the beard and struck him in the face, before he was hurled to the ground and bound hand and foot!

CHAPTER XVI

When the air rests beneath a sleeping sky,
The ocean's surface like a mirror lies:
But when the air is stirred and sky o'ercast,
The angry waters foam before the blast
And hurl their white crests at the lowering skies.

THE unfortunate victim of circumstantial evidence
was placed under guard in the chamber whence he was
taken, daily expecting death and wondering why it
came not. Every hour of his waking moments he
cursed his fate and all who had been instrumental in
leading him to it; but when in the ceaseless round of
malediction, the name of Zaca touched his lips, his voice
failed. If she had doomed him, had he not sworn a
hundred times to himself and to her, that he was ready
to die at her command?

He was young and of small experience with women,
and had never loved before. She had drawn his soul into
hers as the humming-bird draws the nectar of the flowers
and his life existed in her and by her. To believe that
she was faithless was to doubt his loyalty to himself.
To believe that she was as treacherous as the lying
Cazoc made her; that she sought his life with the blood-
thirsty longing of a hungry wolf, was to destroy the

unity of nature—to pull down the sun and roll up the firmament!

Cazoc had lied like a slave—but to what purpose!

If he thirsted for his blood, why had he pulled him out of the jaws of death?

He ground his teeth and wrenched at his bonds, but no light came to his mind; and even as he writhed, the object of his thought stood above him at the distance of three arms' lengths!

At the sight of the monster, his spirit grew calm and he met the sneering laugh of Cazoc with a cold smile of hate!

"What dost thou here, son of Coyoa, lying like a trussed turkey ready for the spit?"

"I am learning patience, good wolf!"

"Thy patience will be no virtue for thou canst do no otherwise! Thou art like a frog caught in the mud where he must remain until the waters come again to crack his shell!"

"I wait for the water!"

Cazoc laughed.

"The water will not come to thee for thy fate is not a moist one! Thou wilt die like a slave! That thou tarriest so long is no mercy, but respect for the law which forbids us to kill in the thirteenth month, as I told thee on the way hither. Thou hast, therefore, three days to live!"

"If they are to be passed in thy company they will

seem cycles! Speak what thou hast to say and begone, so that I may sleep!"

"Thou bearest it bravely, but what I have to say will change thy tune and give thee heart quakes. Thou dost suspect the lady Zaca of treachery and therefore desirest death. Is it not so?"

"What is that to thee?"

"Everything! Food, raiment, air to breathe! Shall the beaver come from his hole and steal the cub of the lion! Shall the grey wolf be mocked by a long-eared hare! I, Cazoc, the son of Chetal, lord of Ilome, love the lady Zaca!"

Tzihn held down his head to conceal the exultation in his face for he knew that he should die triumphant in his love.

"A dog of the south, where the trees rot in the sun and the people live on putrid flesh and the rank oil of palms, has dared to come between me and my love, and therefore, he dies like a dog!"

Every vein in Tzihn's body was bursting with conflicting emotions, but remembering his bonds he restrained his rage and looked calmly up at the scowling visage of his enemy.

Cazoc saw the great peace in his eyes and marveled!

"Thou hast come like a cloud between me and the sun, and the gods have breathed upon thee and thou meltest away! The sages and people of Ilome have leaned upon Cazoc these many years as upon a staff.

When he walked, the earth rose like a rampart to protect his people; when he pointed his spear, death flew like a hawk to a young quail, and prosperity rested in the shadow of his buckler! He had sworn by the urn of his father Chetal to bring the Skystone from the dung heap of Yahvan and restore the daughter of Tzah to her people! Whom among the sons of Ilome could she choose—whom but Cazoc, the valorous, the chief among men? It was written in the stars that it should be so! And thou didst come like a storm at harvest time to spoil the grain—but the gods fettered the storm and gave it doom!

"When thou camest out of Mázacl with Tote, and the cloudburst fell upon thee I was near. I could have suffered thee to drown like a rat, but that I knew thou didst bear a message from the lady Zaca which I wished to read. Because I would save this I rescued thee, and afterwards could not kill thee because of the law. At the rocks thou didst lie upon the pouch as a bird sitteth on an egg, but when thou camest hither I accomplished my purpose. When I had read the tablets I hid them away and told the sages the story thou hast heard, for the desire came to me to see thee die the unknown death!"

"Thou art a liar and a thief!" hissed the prisoner. "Thou hast the vanity of an earth squirrel that sits on a hillock at sundown and measures his height by his long shadow; the voice of a mocking bird, which scares the children with the whine of a wild cat! Thou chatterest like a parrot and hast the antics of an ape! Like a filthy vulture thou waitest until thy prey is in the agony of death, and then thou comest with great flapping wings and greedy yellow eyes, to tear its quivering flesh! Thy spear is a forked tongue; thy buckler deceit and lying, and the spirits of murdered men follow its shadow to send thee to hell when Mazzai, the father of evil, shall call thee home! Where thou treadest the grass withers and yellow toadstools grow, and if the earth rises about thee it is because of its disgust that so foul a thing should live. When he sheds his skin, the snake cometh out of his own mouth—so does thy venomous soul come from between thy lips!

"I spit upon thee, Cazoc the treacherous, and the lady Zaca will loathe and despise thee as I do, for the evil, that is in thee stinks thy skin like the sweat of a slave. And the spirit of Tzihn will be with her and stand between her and thee like a wall of fire. The grey dog shall go forth to die of his own loathsomeness and his bones shall rot where he falls! I, Tzihn, curse thee!"

While he listened Cazoc foamed at the mouth with rage, but restrained himself to the end. Then he loosened the short club that hung at his girdle, and rushed upon the helpless prisoner intending to slay him! As the weapon swung in the air, a hollow voice came from the darkness:

"Thou shalt not kill."

He stayed his hand, remembering the law, and instead gave his enemy a vicious kick.

"Thou carriest thy sting at the end, like a scorpion—but a dead scorpion has no sting!"

Then he left him.

*   *   *   *   *   *   *   *

Tzihn turned his face to the wall and wept, for his spirit was like a ripe bean that opens and drops its seeds upon the ground. When his very soul was melting, a light touch fell upon his shoulder, but he was past sympathy or further suffering and would not turn to see either the face of compassion or the scowl of hate.

"It is I, Popoche, the foster mother of her thou lovest!"

He recalled the woman that sat beside him when he had audience of the sages, and said to himself: She is demented and has neither hate nor love; a fit companion for me now!

"What wilt thou with me, mother?"

She knelt beside him and drew up his head, so that it pressed against her shriveled breast. She wiped his face with a fold of her tunic, crooning like a fond mother over her babe.

"Fear me not," she said, "for the madness has left me. For Zaca whom thou lovest and for him who was consumed in the breath of hell for the crime of the arch-demon Cazoc, Popoche will serve thee. They say I am mad, and well I may be! Sometimes I am. Then my throat is parched; the demons crack stones upon my head and the dead dance before my eyes! Thou lookest like one whom I loved, and the sight of thee has warded off the demons for a season, so that I think clearly and see only those things that make shadows. I know that Cazoc hates thee because thou lovest Zaca; and when he hates, blood drips from his jowls, and Mazzai laughs! Popoche comes to comfort and to serve thee, and thou shalt not die. Listen and be still.

"This chamber has another opening which leads to the cavern of the Urnless Ones, close by the mouth of hell, whose breath is death. Yet there I love to sit waiting for Cazoc, for my soul has called him, and he must come. As I sat, methought I heard the echo of his hated voice, and I came through the darkness and saw him and thee, and thy voice sounded like the voice of the dead when he cursed his enemy. In that instant the clouds were lifted from my mind, and I heard and understood what passed! When his murderous club hung in the air, I remembered the law and cried, 'Thou shalt not kill,' and had he broken it, these hands held a great rock uplifted to dash out his brains! Think quickly, son, for the moments fly—is there aught that Popoche can do?" The hope of life rose in his heart and faded again.

"Mother thou shalt bless me so that my soul shall have wings and live to strew new curses in his path! Like a grasshopper, I shall shed my garment of earth and leaving the shell to men; stretch my new wings and fly to the gods! If thou wilt, treasure this message to the lady Zaca; Tzihn died thinking of her, and his soul waits for its love beyond the clouds!"

He felt hot tears upon his face and they were not his own!

"This I will do, son; but while the heart beats there is hope of life, and the gods never end their work, for where they seem to end, there they begin. If a message were sent to the lady Zaca she could still save thee, perhaps!"

"It is too late, mother!"

"Alas, it is true! Woe, woe! Nor would a message hence be suffered to enter the land of Mázacl."

Then Tzihn remembered that Zaca had hung a curious talisman about his neck when they parted, a yellow stone carved with mystic symbols. He bade Popoche remove it and place it to his lips that he might kiss it, and in the days to come see that it reached her hands.

Popoche did as he wished, and when she took the stone to hide it in her bosom, she saw it closely, and her eyes opened wide in wonder.

With a low cry she rose to her feet and bore it where the light was stronger, and rushing back threw her lean arms about his neck!

"Thou art saved! This is the signet of lord Huema which I have seen a hundred times when he sent messengers to the lord Tzah! Whosoever beareth this into the land of Mázacl shall meet no hindrances, and I know one who has the fleetness of an antelope. He shall carry a message to Yahvan that shall save thee!"

CHAPTER XVII

I come like a bird that flies back to his home-nest;
Spurning the earth like an eagle in flight!
Open the gates of the wonderful star-land—
My soul like a flower follows the light!

AT THE dawn of day, while the stars still glimmered
faintly in the firmament, Popoche crouched upon a flat
rock at the entrance of the valley, and looked along the
path that came from the river, watching for the messenger that had gone to Mázacl.

The stars disappeared one by one, and the rosy
aurora began to tint the sky, flashing from pinnacle to
pinnacle along the mountain tops. The blue smoke rose
behind her from the houses under the cliffs, and the
spirits of night that hid in the low places melted away.

Still none came along the path!

She stretched out her long arms and prayed to the
gods, and when she had finished she saw two forms that
appeared to crawl along the face of the cliff—and one
looked like a bear!

*   *   *   *   *   *   *   *

Upon the morning of the first day of the new year,
Tzihn amoke from a troubled sleep, which was to be his
last upon earth; the two armed men stood beside him.

They unbound his feet and helped him to rise, but his limbs were so numbed that they had to support him. They bore him through a long dark passage into a large chamber lighted by a lamp set upon a pedestal of stone. They placed him against the pedestal and he saw before him dimly a long array of ghostly shapes of men. Withered forms with hollow cavities for eyes. Each held his long hands clasped above his head like a diver preparing for the plunge. Some had fallen upon the floor and were broken into many fragments, so that skulls and trunks and limbs lay at the feet of them that stood upright grinning at their fallen comrades.

He placed his hands before his eyes to shut out the grim figures and strove to imagine what form of death awaited him, that he might prepare to meet it as a warrior should. While he was racking his mind and strengthening his soul one of the men cast down a beam of wood at his feet. They took him and laid him along the beam with his arms crossed above his head, and in this position they bound him with thongs of deer hide. When he was securely fastened they lifted him up and carried him into another chamber, sparely lighted from above, and laid him again upon the ground. He could see nothing but great stalactites that hung from the roof and he wished that one would fall upon him and crush him so as to spare him the horror of the unknown death that awaited him.

While he lay there, Cazoc came, stood over him and put his face against the face of Tzihn and spat upon it!

Tzihn closed his eyes and was silent. Hope was dead in his heart and there was naught left for him to do, but to suffer and die.

When Cazoc had gloated over his victim to his heart's content, the men raised up the beam and bore it to the edge of a great pit whence hot sulphurous air rushed upwards like the breath of a demon and passed through an orifice in the roof to the outer air. They placed the beam upright against the wall of the chamber so that Tzilm could see what death awaited him, and he knew that the beam would be thrown across the mouth of the pit and the hot air would devour the humors of his body and change the soft tissues to parched leather. Afterwards his body would be placed with the other ghostly effigies in the chamber he had left. Yet his spirit was not quenched!

Cazoc fastened a strip of deer skin to the end of his spear and held it over the pit. It curled up like a serpent and shriveled to a ball; and when he had done this he grinned in the face of his victim.

"This is thy death!" he said.

Then he placed his hand to his girdle and hissed in his ear: "These are the tablets which the lady Zaca gave thee! When thou art a mummy I will grind them into powder and salt thee with it!"

But Tzihn heeded him not for his soul was on the

edge of the world; the spirit of the warrior touched his tongue and he sang the death song of the hero:

> "Eu-uh-lieuh! Eu-uh-lieuh!
> Souls of the mighty who dwell in the star-land;
> Shades of my fathers, my spirit is flying!
> Prepare ye a seat for a warrior worthy,
> Whose life is approved by his valor in dying!
>   Eu-uh-lieuh! Eu-uh-lieuh!
> I come like a bird that flies back to his home-nest,
> Spurning the earth like an eagle in flight;
> Open the gates of the wonderful star-land,
> My soul like a flower, turns to the light!
>   Eu-uh-lieuh! Eu-uh-lieuh!
> May my enemies writhe in the clutches of demons—
> Mazzai pursue them and bring them to death!
> I leave them exulting, defiant and mocking—
> With scorn in my heart, and a taunt on my breath!
>   Eu-uh-lieuh! Eu-uh-lieuh!
> By the ghosts of my fathers
> I laugh in their faces
> Their tortures defy!
>   Eu-uh-lieuh! Eu-uh-lieuh!
> They are children and women—
> Unworthy to live—
> Too craven to die!
>   Eu-uh-lieuh! Eu-uh-lieuh!"

Even while he sang they took the beam to throw it across the mouth of hell! The hot blast scorched his body and parched his throat, so that his voice was choked, but while the beam was raised upon their shoulders he saw Cazoc by the side of the pit, and a dark form came from behind, seized him by the middle and cast him headlong into it!

CHAPTER XVII

THE awful fate of Cazoc, and its strange author, so horrified Tzihn's executioners, that they dropped their burden upon the ground and fled in affright.

The voice of him who had done the deed gave their heels wings as he roared after them: "I am Tote, the bison of Mázacl, and when I shake my mane the grey wolves howl and fly to their lairs!"

When they were gone, he pulled Tzihn back from the mouth of the pit where they had dropped him. He unloosed his bonds, placed him upon his feet and gave him the spear of Cazoc which lay upon the ground where he had thrown it after showing Tzihn the death that awaited him; but he himself took up the beam. While he was untying the thongs that bound him to the beam, he told him briefly how the lady Zaca had urged him to go forth into the mountains, for the stars had told her that Tzihn lived! When he was nearing the hills of the giants he was met by Popoche's messenger who told him of Cazoc's treachery and all that followed.

They hurried forward by unfrequented paths and found Popoche awaiting them at the gate of the valley. She showed him a secret entrance to the chamber of the Urnless Ones, and he had arrived in time to send Cazoc to hell!

"Canst thou walk?" he asked.

Tzihn shook his head and leaned heavily upon the spear.

"Then we shall stay together for what the gods shall send, but hold thy spear so that it will look as if it had life!"

While he spoke, there fell upon their ears the noise of a great company approaching, and many warriors entered the chamber, and behind them gleamed the white beards of sages.

Tzihn gritted his teeth and held his weapon like a warrior; and in the dim light no one could see that it wavered like an arrow-weed in the wind. Tote raised the beam above his head and swung it as if it had been a club. His big eyes flamed and his teeth grinned like a wild dog's! The warriors paused at sight of him, thinking him a demon come out of the pit, and their voices were hushed in terror, so that naught was heard but the sound of choking air that came from the throat of Ketecla!

The silence was broken by the hunchback. He lowered an end of the beam to the ground and cried:

"I am Tote the bison of Mázacl! Who touches me dies with his death song unsung!"

His voice broke the spell, for there were many that now recognized him. They advanced upon the two men—but the lord Tacantla came from behind and bade them halt.

When Tote saw him, he asked: "Art thou the lord Tacantla?"

"I am he!"

"Knowest thou me?"

"I take thee for Tote, the renegade, the cousin of the lady Zaca! By birth a lord of Ilome of the house of Tzah and by the curse of the gods a monster—a follower of Lionhead and an enemy of thy people!"

"Thou hast mixed truth and falsehood so well, good uncle, that I cannot answer thee, nor is the time come to do so. Is it peace between us?"

"First, tell me thy business here."

"That I will do in a few words, for this is a choking air and I wish to leave it. The lady Zaca, thy natural chief and ruler, sent me hither to succor her friend, whom thou hast unjustly condemned to death in defiance of her wishes. For this am I here!—obeying when those who have sworn to obey prove traitors to their vows!"

There was a low murmur of voices and Tacantla looked about him anxiously and stroked his beard, fearing to answer before the people.

"What hast thou done with Cazoc?" he asked.

"I have sent him home!" and the speaker pointed to the pit which gurgled and gasped like a narrow-necked gourd that loses its water.

"I have sent him home because he was a thief and a liar and sought to work evil between the lady Zaca and her people!"

"Thou shouldst have demanded judgment against him!"

"I have sent him to those whose judgment is finer than that of men, and will answer for what I have done to her whom I obey!"

"Nay thou shalt answer to us! The lady Zaca is in the hands of the enemy and has no power of judgment. Sages of Ilome is not this the law?"

"I know little of the law, but this beam is a shrewd counsellor and the spear in the hands of Tzihn lacks not cunning. If we fall, it shall be on top of a great heap of dead and dying men!" and Tote advanced a few paces swinging the beam.

The lord Tacantla held a hurried consultation with the sages, and then turned to Tote and said:

"Thou art of the blood of Tzah, although unworthy, and for this reason we will give thee fair trial. If thy cause is just thou hast naught to fear!"

"And what of the stranger?"

"He is condemned already."

"By the gods!" roared Tote in anger, "this shall not

be! If my cause is just he is condemned unjustly, for they are one."

This placed the sages on the horn of a dilemma, for the reasoning of the hunchback was beyond contradiction.

Therefore the lord Tacantla pledged his word that both should be judged together.

Now Tzihn was opposed to yielding, but Tote prevailed over him, feeling that valor, under the circumstances, was best displayed in taking the only path to liberty even though it was narrow and dangerous.

"We consent!" he replied and raised the beam above his head and cast it into the pit.

The breath of the pit sank back with great sobs, and the earth trembled and cracked. There came a roar like the rush of a tempest and a spray of rocks belched forth and fell back. Another great indraught followed, succeeded by an explosion more dreadful than the first, and the beam that Tote had cast in, shot up like an arrow from a bow, and with it came the shrivelled form of a man with his hair standing up like the leaves of the spear plant!

For an instant, while the eye could see and no longer, they danced together in the air, like moving shadows on a rock!

A cry of horror came from those that beheld, but above all rose the shrill scream of a woman!

Popoche, with madness in her eyes, rushed out of the shadow towards the pit, and when she reached the brink, she fell—crushed beneath the beam and the dry husk of Cazocl.

CHAPTER XIX

OUT of the jaws of Ketecla flow ruddy rays of light, when the sages build their council fires at night!

The people who dwell below the cliffs turn their heads upwards like fowls when they see a hawk, and mutter, "Wisdom sits in the mouth of the dead!"

But the stars twinkle on the breast of the night and whisper to each other, We know! We know!

*   *   *   *   *   *   *   *

The sages of Ilome sat in judgment!

The pillars of stone that stood like teeth in the open jaws of Ketecla, lightened in the red flame of the fires; and between them hung the starry firmament like a curtain.

The dry shell of him that was Cazoc lay under a robe near a tall pillar that rose from the floor of the chamber to the roof, and beside it sat the lord Zochapan, who would speak for the dead.

Tzihn and Tote came, guarded by warriors, and stood before the sages.

They swore, by their gods, to speak truly and to the wronging of no man; but the lord Zochapan was not sworn, being the voice of the dead whose spirit could not be bound.

When all was ready, Zochapan whose tongue was like split glass, arose and lifted the robe so that all might see the gnarled and knotted trunk of the dead.

"Where is the grey wolf of the mountains; the scourge of Mázacl; the right arm of Ilome?

"Where is he whose valor exceeded that of the sons of men, as the moon outshines the stars; whose spear was forked lightning and his arrow the thunderbolt?

"Whose voice in war was the roar of the tempest, and in peace, the counsel of a god?

"Has he fallen in battle, drunk with the red glory of war—or passed he away singing his exultant death-song in the teeth of quailing enemies?

"Do we meet to-night to honor his virtues, to chant his praises; to anoint his body with oil for the urn-fire?

"No!

"We are here to judge between him and his murderers! Behold, I drop the robe, for the sight of his corpse will blister our eyes until we have done him justice!

"He has returned from the bowels of the earth to bear witness against them! The gods sent him to testify and demand justice, for who save he ever returned from the pit? What better evidence of his innocence is required than this? Yet, O sages, that all men may admire our justice and mercy, we judge the judgment of the gods themselves!

"Who are his accusers? One comes from the ends of the earth, under the guise of a merchant, to steal the Skystone, the gift of Heaven, the heritage of Ilome. He has confessed it and is by that confession condemned! Still we plead for judgment! He has lifted his eyes to the daughter of Tzah! He has dishonored the face of the lord Tacantla with a foul blow! He has plucked at the beard of wisdom and smitten the people through their law!

"He claims to be a friend of the lady Zaca when we know that she sent him hither to be judged for his iniquities.

"He was adjudged to death and yet he lives to mock us! He claims that he was sent here with a message. Where is it—who has seen it? He who is dead told you that he had no message, and his words were found to be true. O, sages, words are like clouds that cover the face of the sun:

"And the other—he claims to be of our blood and yet he has fought against us, allied with our enemies! What mercy shall be shown to the fratricide? Shall I light a torch in the sunlight that ye may see? The two are leagued together for evil to Ilome, but the anger of the gods is kindled against them. They have charged us to rid the earth of this monster, whose shadow blights the earth, whose hideous shape if seen will cause our women to bear things like him!

"Judgment, O sages, judgment!"

When he had finished, an angry murmur filled the chamber and several of the warriors raised their clubs above the heads of the strangers menacing them with death. The sages whispered in the ear of lord Tacantla, casting ominous looks upon the prisoners, but he shook his head, and waved his hand to the warriors so that they fell back.

Tote and Tzihn knew then that they were already judged, and that if they were permitted to speak in their own behalf it would be a mere formality. If there had been any uncertainty regarding this it was settled by the manner of the lord Tacantla when he called upon Tote to answer for his cause.

"Out of our mercy," he said, "which, like the sun, shines for all, we permit thee to speak for thyself and him who is already condemned, but have a care that the privilege be not abused!"

Tote gathered his hair into a knot upon his head, like a warrior preparing for the fray, and smiled in the face of Tzihn, as if to say, Thou shalt see great things!

He advanced to the pillar of rocks, that rose in the center of the chamber like the trunk of a tree. There he raised his eyes to the roof as if rapt in meditation, and the men marveled that he showed so little fear.

When he spoke it was with the voice of one who is weary and wishes to sleep.

"O sages, what is truth? Is it a lie twice told?

"Shall the falsehoods of Cazoc become purged of their poison by much repeating? The lord Zochapan is the echo of a lie, and the echo of a lie is but a lie twice told!

"What shall I answer to the accusations against us? If I speak the truth ye will not hear it, for your ears are stopped with lies; and if I am silent, ye will say that I fear to answer. Though my strength is in my arms, I too can work my jaws, so that my lips froth like the lord Zochapan's, but froth is no more wisdom than it is the white frost, and the soap weed can froth to more purpose than either of us!

"This great hump upon my shoulders is more eloquent than my tongue for it has power to pull down this pillar against which I lean—if it were not so firmly rooted! I have told you that I was sent by the lady Zaca to find Tzihn who had been accounted dead. As there is peace between us, I brought no message from her. I found him in a dire extremity and with him its author, that liar and thief, Cazoc.

"If she lived, Popoche would bear witness to our innocence, but she is dead—like Cazoc!

As to the tablets, Zaca told me that she gave them to Tzihn, and if they are lost, Cazoc stole them!"

He paused, as if considering what he should say next,

and leaned heavily against the pillar, smiling at Tzihn.

And then Tzihn understood what his purpose was, and smiled back at him, but the sages and warriors scowled upon them both and raised their voices against them.

"Peace!" cried Tacantla, "let him speak till his tongue is weary!"

"If the gods wished to return Cazoc to earth," continued Tote in the same calm tone, "why did they first suck out his soul? It looks to me, O sages, as if the gods touched him not, but the demons of the pit spewed him up because he was too vile for hell!"

A shout of rage came from the warriors, and none heard the sharp cracking of the roof which had been loosened by the shaking of the cliff when the pit choked —none but Tote and Tzihn.

When the angry outcry subsided, Tote resumed; but now his voice rose like a battle cry.

"Think not, O sages, that Tote trembles before you! It may be true that the sight of me will make your women bear monsters, for your warriors have often changed to rabbits before me! I am Tote, the bison of Mázacl, and fear no death that ye can invent! I defy ye all! I roar against ye like the wind that runneth before the rain! I blow curses into your faces like hot scorching sand! O sages, O fools! see ye not that the choking giant cracked the roof of the chamber? This pillar alone holds back the scaly rock and with these arms and shoulders I will hurl it down and let destruction fall upon ye!"

Tote had thrown his arms about the pillar and his great shoulders and hump rose with swelling muscles, and Tzihn stood by his side!

Terror seized them all so that they stirred not; only Zochapan pulled the robe from the body of Cazoc and covered himself with it.

Large boulders broke loose from the pillar and fell upon the floor and the cracks in the roof widened, yet none fled, for terror and amazement held them rooted where they stood.

The voice of Tacantla broke the silence.

"What will ye?" he asked.

"That we go free!"

At that moment Tzihn remembered how Cazoc at the pit had boasted that he carried the tablets at his girdle. When Zochapan pulled off the robe that covered the body, it had turned slightly, exposing to view the shrivelled pouch.

This Tzihn saw and he tore open the scorched leather and found the tablets intact.

He held them up and cried: "Behold the tablets that were stolen from me! The gods have sent back the dead to do justice to the living!"

CHAPTER XX

Who would now bear the Skystone over plain and hill, through desert and forest, to the people of Coyoa?

The gods had warred against Naqua, the last green limbs of hope were withered, and desolation blackened his heart.

The end of his life was crowned with thorns and remorse lashed his soul.

Grief consumed him; his flesh shrank to the bone; his blood moved like slimy water over a newly plowed field; his sight failed, and his mind wavered at times like a bat in the sunlight. The hour-stick of his days was fanned by the breath of Mazzai, the evil one, so that it burnt fast like a wisp of straw. Success gilds sin so that the foul methods are unseen, but failure adds to their iniquity. He forgot the glory of self-sacrifice and remembered only the means by which it was to be achieved. Remorse seized him like a python and crushed his spirit in its folds. Day and night it tightened about him and the tender sympathy of lord Huema added poignancy to the sting of conscience.

For several days he lay upon his back, seeing nothing but the blackness of his ingratitude.

Should he die and say nothing of the great wrong purposed against the laws of hospitality and the bond of friendship, or should he ease his conscience by a full confession and make what expiation might be demanded of him? If he was forgiven, he would pass over to his fathers in peace with a smile upon his face and light in his heart—and if it were otherwise, death could not come too quickly!

The cross of Azzu, that rules the southern sky appeared to him, as in a dream. And behold, the stars rushed together and formed one central orb whose refulgence dazzled his eyes. Out of the midst of the glory, a voice spoke to his soul; the voice of Azzu, who suffered for men; and he understood, and peace fell upon him!

*   *   *   *   *   *   *   *

The lord Huema came to him when he sent, and placed his hand upon his fevered brow and blessed him.

Then the heart of Naqua swelled with love, and with his hands clasped over his breast, he told him all.

"Thou knowest," he said, "how our people parted at the Cities of the Lakes, some to the north and some to the south, and others, following Mázacl, came hither after many wanderings. Those that went to the south bore with them the eye of Tzebu, the twin of that which is called the Skystone, and while they had this, prosperity was their handmaiden and peace their evening and morning star. They raised their dwellings as you come to the Black Hills, that hold the earth together, dividing the east from the west; by wide lakes that reminded them of their former home; and their generations filled the land. After many cycles, they, like the people of Mázacl strayed from the faith of their fathers and followed their own vain fancies. Dissensions sprang up among their chief men, but the people still clung together and their harvests never failed.

"But the curse came upon them when they warred with each other, brother against brother and father against son.

"Then the lakes were rolled up like dry palm leaves in the sun, and borne on the air to the mountains whence they returned filled with evil spirits, and fell upon the land in a deluge. The grasshoppers and locusts came from the north like clouds of dust on the desert and no green thing remained when they had passed. The people cursed each other and strove to excel in evil, following those whose tongues were bitterest. They scattered like the seed of the cotton-wood in a storm, some wandering to the north, and some to the south and west. In that time of trouble, the eye of Tzebu disappeared. Each faction seized that which it could lay hands upon, and whether it went to the north or west I know not, but it went not with my people.

"I am of those that settled by the great western sea, near the Breasts of Coyoa, where the cross of Azzu flames in the midnight sky. For a time we increased and multiplied upon the savannahs and the hills. But after many generations, those that lived in the lowlands quarreled with their brethren of the hills and crossed the mountains to dwell by the eastern sea. There they built great temples of rock and flourish to this day, for I have visited them.

"When they were gone, the White Spirit settled upon the Breasts of Coyoa and the curse fell! Our women were barren or bore few children; the spotted plague came to us and the red-blight to the corn; the god of storms lived in the mountains and hurled down the cliffs upon our homes and fields. Yet the people clung together and waited for Azzu to come! While I was yet a young man, the sages remembered the genius of our race, the eye of Tzebu and the tradition of how it was lost to us. They decided that its restoration would alone abate the curse and urged me to go in quest of it.

"I had traveled much, and the desire to see strange peoples and scenes was strong in me. I agreed to journey to the north, whence our fathers had come, and try to recover the precious gem. With a great store of merchandise and many slaves, I began my journey, followed for many days by sons of Coyoa; but when we reached the great plains beyond the mountains I dismissed them, for I judged that our numbers might anger the tribes who as a general rule molest not the simple merchant. I saw the walls of the temples and houses our fathers had built, but the land was a desert.

"I turned to the west, and after six days met a company of traffickers returning from the north who told me of a people that dwelt on a fertile plain between two rivers. They described them as a cultivated race who built great temples and granaries and understood many arts. What interested me most was the statement that they worshipped the eye of their god, which they called the Skystone, for I knew then that they must be a remnant of my own race. I came to the borders of the land of Mázacl, and my heart sank when I found that I could not pass beyond; but the service I was able to render thee removed the barrier, and I came to Yahvan.

"Little didst thou guess my errand, or thou wouldst have cast me out naked and bruised! Thy kindness gave me many opportunities to steal the gem, but ever as they came, my spirit failed me. Thy love made the deed seem an outrage—and so the time slipped by. The longer I remained the weaker my resolution became, and at last I resolved to return to my people and tell them that the eye of Tzebu was irrevocably lost.

"I found that the curse had lightened in my absence, and for several years prosperity smiled upon us. Mazzai mocked us for a season, and when his wrath was again loosed against us, the cry of the people pierced my heart! With dirt upon my head, I told the sages that I had lied when I said the eye of Tzebu was lost! I confessed all to them, and they bade me go forth again with a band of chosen warriors, and return not without the treasure.

"The bodies of those that came with me, rest far from their homes. They died like heroes and had the sepulture of dogs!

"And now Tzihn is gone, the noblest and bravest of them all—victim of the storm-god—crushed like a weed between the rolling rocks, his fragments scattered so that no man shall know their resting place! Death has taken the young and the brave and despised old Naqua! Let my sin be accounted against me in thy heart as the crime of a loving mother who offers all that she has for her children!"

*　　*　　*　　*　　*　　*　　*　　*

Lord Huema paced the floor of the chamber for several minutes in deep thought, and then stopped by the couch of Naqua, and spoke as one that argues with himself:

"Does length of years bring wisdom, or is it the vanity of age to think that it is wise? The frog has no wisdom and yet when the earth is parched, he hides in the dust; and when the rains fall, he comes forth and croaks his joy! The frog seeks not to rule the seasons, and the ant knows that in winter there is no harvest. Man seeks for signs and prodigies and reaches out for a guiding hand.

"When the sun scorches, he lolls in the shade of trees and prays for the cold breath of winter. When winter comes, he hugs the warm fire and sighs for summer! We pretend to read the stars and hold communication with the gods, yet lack the patience of the brute. The child profits by correction, but man resents it, and rails against fate because the laws of nature are not stayed in his behalf. If the storm destroys his little field or undermines the foundation of his house, so that it falls, he cries against the storm-god. If he quarrels with his brother and is worsted, the gods are made responsible.

"He forgets that without the storms the channels of the rivers would become dry, the clouds be barren of moisture, and his harvests never come. He remembers only the harm they do and has no thought of the good. In the heat of his passion and the distraction of his mind, he provokes his brother, and because the whip that he makes scourges him, he is wroth with the gods because they do not abandon heaven to wreak his vengeance.

"Thus we reach above the clouds for things that hang upon our eyelids like our tears, but are unseen like these, because our eyes are closed with the rheum of passion! Let us forget the vanity of wisdom and judge fairly if the gods have really afflicted man, or man's transgressions have brought him sorrow.

"Our people lived in peace and harmony for ages by the great lakes, and the Skystone was with them. Nevertheless they fell into error and mocked the teachings of their prophets. They quarreled first because the demon of discord moved them, having no cause, except differing opinions that were all wrong. When the hair-splitting disease had run its term like a fever of the blood, they disputed as to who among them was the legitimate guardian of the Skystone.

"This being a strife with a definite object, they warred with each other like dogs over the carcass of a deer, and broke up into factions, their hate intensified by their kinship.

"Peace abandoned the land, and many of the people unable to endure the strain of constant warfare sought new homes at a distance, some leaving before the catastrophe that overwhelmed the Cities of the Lakes and others going forth afterwards, as did the followers of Mázacl. In the confusion of that time of terror, when the earth seemed to rise in the air and the waters fled, the stone came into the possession of the leaders of thy people, to curse them with strife. The Skystone neither provoked the evil nor stayed it, and we must infer that it was either powerless or indifferent.

"When your people dwelt by the Black Hills, prosperity attended them until they warred with each other over the stone as their ancestors had done. Its loss preceded not, but followed their transgressions. The favor of the gods was not withdrawn from them until they had forfeited it.

"I have told thee of the defection of Ilome and its destruction because of the ambition of its sages to become the guardians of the gem, and the time may come when the same cause will rend the peace of Mázacl!"

"O lord," cried Naqua, "there is truth in thy words, and a child should see these things!"

"Wisdom," replied Huema, "runneth after fables, and the wit of a child is often shrewder than the deep thought of age. The vanity of learning obscures our outward vision so that we see nothing but what is within us. If thou hast followed me, thou seest now that in seeking the Skystone for the redemption of thy people, thou hast been guilty of a folly, for redemption cometh from within, as the growth of our bodies.

"The curse upon thy people must be the result of natural causes, for the gods can have no spite against men! When thou camest to Mázacl first I soon perceived thy errand, and watched the workings of thy mind. I loved thee for thy resistance to the command of a duty that impelled thee to violate the rites of hospitality and prove thyself an ingrate; and when thou didst depart I looked for thee to return!"

Naqua covered his face with his hands and wept, for such generosity opened the fountains of his soul.

"Why should I upbraid thee now! The Skystone which we have is that which belonged to thy people and thou didst but seek thine own!"

Naqua raised himself upon his elbows and through his tears looked at the speaker, who smiled down upon him.

"It is the truth that I speak, O Naqua!"

"I thought it was the twin of that which was lost, for our traditions referred to two of equal size and power."

"There was only one, for in the ancient writings that I have shown thee, its history is given. The great Tzebu was descended from a race of kings who lived in the land where the sun sleeps, and the gem was one of the treasures that he bore with him when he fled across the waters. He valued it as the emblem of the nobility of his race and it had no other virtue.

"He wore it in a gorget upon his breast, and when he went up into the mountain to die, so that no man should know his grave, he bestowed it upon his successor as a symbol of office and commanded the people that when they saw the great stone they should remember him who though invisible yet watched over their welfare. From a mere badge of office and a memento of the Founder of our race, it became in course of time, the real presence of a god, with the power of life and death.

"When your people dispersed at the Black Hills, some came to the land of Mázacl bringing with them the gem. Being of kin they were made free of the land upon the condition that they deposited their treasure in the temple and made no claim thereto. This they did, and intermingled with our people so that their identity was almost lost. But I fear that the day will come when some among them will remember, as did the lord Tzah, that they brought the Skystone into the land, for he was of thy people; therefore I hold it as a curse, and if it were not for the people, who esteem it as their souls, I would destroy it!

"For many years I have shown only the casket that holds it in order that the sight of it might not provoke envy or stir ambitious minds, giving as a reason, that since the rebellion of Ilome its safety is thus best assured."

"Thou hast done well!"

CHAPTER XXI

ZACA was restless and sick at heart for Tote returned not.

She walked under the trees and watched the yellow water in the canal play with the shadow. The red leaves and the brown fluttered about her like butterflies, and the rising wind soughed and whistled through the gaunt limbs of the trees.

Impelled by a feverish desire to be alone with her thoughts, she commanded the slave that accompanied her, to return, and she walked on until the summit of the temple shone above the trees like a far off cloud.

The fever left her and she felt weary and wished she had not strayed so far. It was a lonely spot on a rising ground above the level of the canal, and so sterile as to be unfit for cultivation. For some time she looked in vain for a habitation where she might rest and refresh herself, and the barrenness of the place oppressed

At last she espied a small house in a hollow, and although it was uninviting she resolved to go to it and ask for a drink of water.

She approached and called aloud at the door, but no answer came, and she lifted the mat and entered. The place appeared to be deserted, but seeing a jar of water with a gourd cup by its side, she served herself. Prompted by curiosity she raised the mat of the door that led beyond and looked into a yard enclosed with high walls of concrete. In the middle of the yard sat a girl feeding some birds, and she walked towards her. Then she saw that the child's body was bent and twisted, and the arms, bare to the elbow, were skin and bone. There was a singular sweetness in her pinched face and she chattered merrily in strange language to the feathered flock. Some of them were lame, with broken limbs and twisted bodies like her own, and these she kept near her and fed with her hands or from her mouth, and they answered her with sounds like those she made.

Doves came from afar and lighted upon the wall; and when she saw them she called them in sweet piping tones, and after hesitating a moment they joined the motley throng about her. Occasionally a robust bird became jealous of the attention shown the cripples and pecked at them. Then the girl's lips pursed up and she seized the offender and lectured it severely. When she turned it loose again, it walked off spiritless and ashamed and would not eat until she called it to her and caressed it.

Zaca marveled at what she saw and drew near to the child.

The eyes that rose to meet hers appeared to look into her soul and she felt abashed as in the presence of greatness. Yet the child was only a poor cripple— hanging to life like a bruised flower upon the stem, and like the flower exhaling a fragrance that perfumed the air.

What effect her sudden appearance had upon the child she could not guess. There was no change in her countenance showing astonishment or fear. She gazed at her calmly for a few moments, a bird in each hand, and then asked, "What art thou?"

Zaca was dumb, knowing not what answer to make to this strange question.

"Thou art one of the fair spirits the Wunksh has spoken of. Thy face is beautiful as the sunrise, thy hair like the big clouds that hide the sun, and thou hast the breast and wings of a white pigeon. Oh, thou art a strange bird come from the south where the green parrots live!"

"I am not a bird."

"Thou wearest feathers like birds!"

"I am a woman!"

"How can that be? Chácama is a woman, and her face has the color of burnt corn, her hair is like the bear skin that I sleep upon, and she wears a brown tunic of fibre cloth."

"Indeed I am a woman."

The child was puzzled, but not having learned to doubt, believed.

"The Wunksh sent thee?"

"I know not whom thou meanest. I came to rest and drink, and finding no one about, I entered. Who is that thou namest?"

"Wunksh is—Wunksh! Every one loves him, he is so beautiful and strong—not so beautiful as thou art, for he has no feathers. What art thou called?"

"Zaca!"

"That is not the name of a bird! But it is a sweet one and I shall love it if Wunksh does!"

"And thy own name, little one?"

"Shingladee!"

"That is no name—it is the voice of a bird when it cries to its mother. How camest thou by it?"

"The birds gave it me. Wunksh can say it!—not as the birds do though."

"Canst thou understand what the birds say?"

"That I can. See this linnet that pecks at my ear and works his wings and peeps! He is impatient to know who thou art, and I will tell him and send him to kiss thee."

She took the bird in her hand, put its beak near to her mouth and uttered short whistling sounds. Then she placed it down and it flew upon the shoulder of Zaca and ruffled its wings and cried "Peep!"

"What didst thou say to it?"

"That thou wast a shingladee-wunksha-wunksh!"

"What does that mean?"

The little one was perplexed.

"I cannot tell thee except that it has convinced him that thou art a lover of birds and will do him no harm. Perhaps he believes thou art some strange bird, as I did, for see how he chirps to thy feathers! Now, I will call that great turkey who struts and spreads his wings because the linnet has been preferred.

"Wunkshidee-Wunksh!"

The bird stopped and looked at her from under his red tassels.

"Wunkshidee!"

He closed his wings and came to her and poked his mottled head into her lap. She whispered to him and he stalked solemnly over to Zaca, rustling his wings and puffing himself out as if to say, We are fine birds and ought to know each other!

Zaca laughed and wondered.

"I will teach thee to call the birds!"

And Zaca tried to imitate the strange sounds that came from her little mouth but she only made noises that frightened the birds, whereat they both laughed.

The sun now began to fail and the air grew chilly.

"I am cold!" said the little one, "and wish to lie

upon the bear-skin and think of Wunksh! Chácama comes not, and yet she said she would stay but a few moments to gather some herbs for the aches that come to her bones in winter. I know what they are, for I have them always. But thou wilt not tell Wunksh—Zaca!" and she looked into her face entreatingly.

"Why shouldst thou hide it from him?"

"It would give him pain to know that I suffer, and I love him."

Zaca humbled her spirit before such a love and asked tenderly, "Canst thou not walk?"

"Oh yes, I can walk—when Wunksh is by—but it hurts me! Chácama will be here presently. I will send my Wunkshidees to bed!"

She clapped her hands and cried Wunksha-wunksh—with an intonation different from any she had given, and the birds raised their heads and went to their roosts, all save two cripples which she held in the skirt of her tunic.

"Can I not carry thee to the house?" asked Zaca.

The girl's eyes brightened with pleasure.

Zaca lifted her up with her birds and she seemed to have no weight. There was nothing of her but her long thick hair and dreamy eyes. Her heart beat like a frightened bird's and her breath was so short that Zaca trembled, but the little one smiled in her face and she was relieved.

When they were inside, the girl asked Zaca to place

her feathered invalids in a corner of the room in a warm nest of feathers, which she did, and was turning away with the child in her arms when the mat of the outer door was raised and Tote stood before them!

"Wunksh!"

"Shingladee!" and he stretched out his arms and took her to his heart. Her arms stole about his neck and her head rested upon his shoulder.

"Zaca, what dost thou here?"

"I came by chance. What is this child to thee?"

"My life, my soul! Ask me not now. Rest thee a moment and I will return and tell thee!"

He bore his frail burden into another room, and as they went, the little one patted his cheek and caressed him and he buried his face in her hair.

From where she stood Zaca heard them converse in low, sweet tones like lovers.

"Wunksh! Shingladee! Wunksh!"

*   *   *   *   *   *   *   *

He returned and stood before her and there was a radiance in his face that Zaca could not understand.

"First," he said, "I will tell thee of Tzihn."

Her lips trembled, but her voice was firm as she answered: "As thou wilt."

"He is well."

Her head fell upon her bosom so that he saw not her face when she asked:

"Where is he?"

"He comes speedily, but I came faster. Wilt thou hear how it fared with him?"

She raised her head and with a soft light in her eyes, said, "No—let us talk of the child!"

Tote looked at her bewildered, not understanding the moods of women.

"Who is she that talks to birds, and calls thee and herself by names that are not human?"

"Sit thee down, cousin, and I will tell thee her story!

*   *   *   *   *   *   *   *

"I found her when she was an infant, lying abandoned in the field. She was wrapped in a coarse cloth and asleep. Wondering what the bundle could be I opened it. She awoke and her eyes drew me down to her until my face touched hers, and a sweet music sang in my soul! Her tiny hands fumbled at my throat; then twined about my neck, and she became a part of me, soul of my soul and life of my life!

"No one was near, nothing but the birds and the whispering leaves and grass. I lifted her up and bore her to this place, and she fell asleep again as I walked. I laid her down and sought the slave Chácama, and bade her care for the child and tell no one but her husband, on her life!

"These two lived in the house and nurtured her until Chácama's husband died, and then she was alone. I had a wall built about it so that there was no entrance save by the door of the house and gave command that no stranger should be suffered to enter.

"What I did provoked no surprise for I was known to have strange moods, and to love solitude. When Chácama examined the infant she said that it was a helpless cripple; not merely deformed as I am, but one whose life would be a burden and to whom death would come as a blessing. At first I wished that she might die and cease to suffer; but she lived and twined about my heart until I knew that when she died the light of my life would go out, and her ashes would be the ashes of my soul!

"Oh Zaca, when she lies upon my breast thou canst not imagine what I see and hear. The world is beautiful and the air full of ravishing sounds. When I am away from her my spirit is heavy and the world is dark, and I count the moments until I return. For her I have valued my life and treasured this ugly shape, which to her is grace and beauty, for she sees that in me which I have not to other eyes than hers. When I am alone, her spirit comes to me and drives the evil spirits away, and lifts my soul above the shadows of my thoughts!"

"She is a strange child! Hast thou discovered aught of her parentage?"

"I have guessed it, as thou canst too!"

"The child of a slave mother! Then, by the law, she shall die!"

"I know the law. For this reason I have hidden her these many years. But the law shall not touch her. She is of the gods and above the law. The spirit of a star has inhabited her frail body, and when she dies thou wilt see a new light in the firmament. And if it were not so, I, Tote, stand between her and the law, like a fierce fire of stubble after the harvest! Who touches her dies, though it were the lord Huema himself! I will rend him limb from limb, and tear his flesh from his bones like a wolf!

"Tote asks nothing of man, but to be let alone. This star gem is all he has, and it shall not be taken from him —except by the gods!"

CHAPTER XXII

SHE knew that he was coming for her heart choked her breath, and a strange light, like falling stars, filled the air.

In a few moments, he came and stood before her!

He stopped, panting like a startled deer, and looked at her with devouring eyes.

He fainted with the desire to hold her against his heart, but the ravishment of joy within his reach overmastered him, and he stood like a boy that holds the luscious fruit he craved and feeds upon anticipation!

Which moved towards the other first, neither could tell, but space failed between them and their desire was crowned with the ecstacy of meeting!

*   *   *   *   *   *   *   *

He told her how he had been rescued from the waters by Cazoc and conducted to the hills; of his strange reception there and all that followed.

"When I discovered the tablets upon the body of Cazoc everything was changed. They were read and understood and all men knew then that the dead had lied. Judgment was pronounced against him and his dry shell consigned to the chamber of the Urnless Ones!"

"His was an awful doom!" said Zaea. "My flesh creeps at the thought of it, and yet it was the one that he had designed for thee.

"Popoche, too! She was my foster mother, Tzihn— and from her breast I drew life giving food! Five years ago she fled from Mázacl to the hills, and having left of her own free-will, could not return. She loved me—and some powerful motive must have drawn her from my side!"

"I heard her story from the mouth of one that loved her too, he who took the message that brought Tote to my aid. She had a son who followed Cazoc. He was condemned to die the nameless death for a grievous crime. Popoche fled to the hills to intercede for him, but arrived too late—he was dead! When the first spasms of her grief were over, her interest in the world was no more than that of a blasted tree that stands erect and throws a shadow from the sun. But a change took place when she learnt that her son had suffered without guilt; that it was the crime of Cazoc himself, who, to conceal his own infamy, fastened it upon her son and pursued him to death!"

"Oh, monster that he was!"

"Then her mind, already weakened with grief, gave

way, save the hate of Cazoc lived like a coal of fire. I reminded her in some manner of her son, and the sensations this fancy aroused, lifted the cloud from her mind for a season, and death followed!"

"Alas, Popoche!"

"Afterwards," continued Tzihn, "the lord Tacantla made all things clear to me."

"He is a fox for cunning," observed Zaca, "and like a fox knows when to hide! What said he?"

"Cazoc had been the soul of their schemes, the staff upon which they leaned and they feared that his loss at this critical time would ruin the cause. It was their hope that thou wouldst become his wife!"

Zaca frowned and said: "Go on—what more?"

"This had been given some color by Cazoc, for he claimed to enjoy thy favor, and hinted of a secret understanding to this intent!"

"He was a false villain and deserved to die for this, if for nothing else! I love Tote for what he did!"

"Nevertheless, when he told his story, it seemed more than probable to those whose minds were inflamed with his lies!"

"What was the story?"

"That thou wert angered because I lifted mine eyes to thee; that thou didst lure me to the hills with false hopes, to be adjudged and condemned there; that thou didst so tell Cazoc, and gave me no tablets in order that the matter might be plain!"

"Didst thou doubt me, Tzihn?"

"Evil spirits came to me when I cursed, and said, Curse her who betrayed thee with the rest! But ever as thy name came to my lips, I felt thy breath upon my cheek, the air was full of great swimming eyes—and my lips froze together and the curse rattled in my throat like a dying breath. The agony of that time when it returns to memory, covers my body with a cold, clammy dew! When Cazoc came to taunt me, he reached too far and toppled over. His unruly tongue gave out the truth! Then I smiled in his face and heeded not what he said except to deride his hate. Peace came to me as to the bird under his mother's wing. I knew that Zaca loved me, and I died for her!"

"O Tzihn thou art dearer to me than my life, and for every pang thou hast suffered, the gods shall give thee bliss!"

*   *   *   *   *   *   *   *

"I see through the arts of Tacantla," said Zaca. "He is too shrewd to have been misled by the wiles of Cazoc. As he ruled my father, the Tzah, so he governed Cazoc, and hoped through thy death to remove an obstacle from his path. He knew well enough that I loved thee, but because that love might interfere with his plans, he would destroy thee—trusting to make his peace with me thereafter.

"When Cazoc was dead his busy mind ran to new plans. He spared thee and Tote by the pit in order that he might have time to think! I doubt much that he would have injured thee, even if the tablets had not been found, but when they were, his path was made clear. Then he became thy friend, and it is well it is so, for he has power and shrewdness.

"Did he not urge Tote to cast in his lot with them?"

"That he did, but vainly."

"Nothing will shake his fidelity to Mázacl, which is so well proven that he has privileges to go and come accorded to no other of his race. Nothing," added Zaca with a sigh, "but one thing, and that will come when the gods will! What said Tacantla of my plans and why didst thou return so speedily?"

"Thou didst charge the sages to give me their confidence, and as thou didst command, I told them all that was planned with Naqua and asked counsel."

"And their counsel was—"

"That when the time came thou shouldst fly with me to the hills. Thy presence among them will inspire the people with new hope, strengthen their arms, and give substance to their cause. Thou wilt be their Azurath, the queen of victory, the fortunate, the arbiter of destiny, the handmaiden of the sun! Now they have nothing but counsel upon counsel, words of wisdom that consume each other with their own fire! The lord Lionhead is now at Tzanahl, the city of the Two Rivers, trying to pacify the people who are sullen because of the pride of Yahvan and the exactions of the priests.

Coyal is aggrieved because the great canal of Mázacl drains the river in the dry seasons, causing their crops to be so meagre that they have no surplus for trade. These, I learn, are chiefly the descendants of a people that came from the south after the settlement of the land, and are akin to those of Ilome."

"They are indeed of our blood," said Zaca, "but it has been so drugged with that of Mázacl that it runs sluggishly. I, too, am of those that came from the south—but the house of Tzah was undefiled. We brought the Skystone to the land and it was forced from us as the tribute of our necessity!"

"The belief is strong with the sages and people, that thy father is not dead, but a prisoner in the temple."

"This I have heard—but it is not probable."

"The lord Tacantla urged me to learn if Naqua knew aught of the matter."

"If he does, I fear he will not tell thee."

"If he does not, I will enter the temple by the secret passage from the pyramid, which Tote discovered."

"Thou wilt be discovered and delivered to death!"

"Rememberest thou the talisman thou gavest me when we parted, a yellow stone marked with strange characters?"

"I remember."

"The mother Popoche told me that it is the signet of lord Huema with which one may pass freely whithersoever he will! How camest thou by it?"

"Tote stole it from Naqua while he slept, and gave it me!"

"Then Popoche was right, for Naqua himself told me that he had it, and grieved sorely when it was lost. Thou seest now that if Naqua fails me I have the means whereby I can help myself. But that which I have not said, is most important. I leave the best for the last!

"Thou knowest that it was arranged that Naqua should steal the Skystone and give it me to carry to my people—"

"And thus I urged thee to absent thyself about the time the deed was to be done, for I wished not that thou shouldst be tempted. Where thy affections gather thou art easily persuaded! Even now I fear that Naqua will win thee from the cause of Zaca, and thou wilt remember too kindly the home of thy fathers!"

"Rest thy heart, O loved one! It is easier to tear up a mountain by its roots and bear it to the great sea, than to tear thee and thy cause from my heart!"

"May the gods keep thee firm, O Tzihn!"

"Know then that the lord Tacantla sent me hither in haste to urge Naqua to the deed! The Skystone, as thou knowest, is the idol of the people, and they will follow it as the swallow follows the sun! If I take the gem from Naqua, what is to prevent me from flying with it to the hills?—and thou shalt go with me, and it shall bless our nuptials!"

His conscience whispered to his soul so faintly that it was as the buzzing of a fly, Only thine honor shall prevent! But Zaca had her arms about his neck; her lips touched his as the dew kisses the flower, and his conscience slept upon her lips!

CHAPTER XXIII

WHEN Naqua was notified of the return of Tzihn his emotions were of a very conflicting nature. Tzihn had become a memory linked to a crime, and life to the one meant the resurrection of the other. If the memory was painful how much more so was the reality!

The battle he had fought must be waged again, and who could guess the ending!

Tzihn represented the abandoned cause, the cause his reason condemned as unprofitable and his conscience reprobated as evil. He would claim the fulfillment of the vow made to his people and to the gods!

If he told the truth boldly he would appear a traitor who adds cowardice and falsehood to his treason; and if he lied, he would not be believed.

Upon one side stood fidelity to his resolution and gratitude, besides the vows by which he had bound himself to Mázacl; and on the other was his faith pledged to his own people!

The more he debated the matter with himself the

more involved it became, and he resolved finally to see Tzihn and trust to inspiration. Surely the Great God, Huema had made known to him, would remove this obstacle from his path, and let him die in peace!

* * * * * * * *

Naqua went to the chamber of Tzihn in the house of Lionhead, and finding him not there, entered the court to wait for him. He was glad that he had not met him at once, for no light had come to him; and as he walked the path he hid his face in his hands so that his soul could hear a message if one should come.

Voices in low converse fell upon his outward ears.

He dropped his hands and saw Zaca and Tzihn where they sat like two doves in the mating season. He lifted his hands to heaven and gave thanks, for light had come. He retired from the court without being perceived, and calling a slave that passed, bade him tell Tzihn that Naqua awaited him.

* * * * * * * *

"O son," he said to Tzihn when they had kissed, "thou art as one returned from the grave! My soul was sick with agony when the evil news came, and death watched by my couch. But I see thee safe and well and the joy of meeting thee again in life is like the sweet taste of honey after a bitter draught. Let us sit together, and thou shalt tell me of thy strange experience."

Tzihn's heart was grieved to see the great change in his friend. Ten years had been added to his age. His figure had the bent stiffness of decrepitude; his eyes were sunken and rheumy; his visage pinched and wan and the hands he held in his own shook with palsy.

His love returned, and for the moment he forgot all that drew him away from the past. He remembered only the great love between them, and saw in Naqua the spirit of his father and the heart of his people. He recounted briefly all that had befallen him, suppressing only that which Naqua should not know.

When he was finished, the old man kissed him as if he were a child, and tears mingled with the rheum in his eyes.

Then they sat looking at each other for a space, their minds intent upon the same subject. Naqua broke the silence.

"O Tzihn, the time I spoke of went by and thou wert not here."

"I know it, father, but another time will come and here I shall be."

"Is thy resolve firm to return to Coyoa?"

Tzihn bowed his head affirmatively, and drew lines upon the floor with his finger.

"Hast thou thought of the dangers of the way? The desert plains, the fearful mountain paths; the savage beasts and hostile tribes? Canst thou endure the gnaw of hunger and the rage of thirst; the scorching heat and piercing wintry blasts? When we came we were many and our needs provided for, but thou must measure back the endless days of toilsome march alone, without defense or means. My heart faints for thee, for I fear that thou wilt perish in the way!"

His voice was full of entreaty and Tzihn was puzzled, suspecting not the truth.

"O father," he said, "thou hast faithfully called up before my eyes the hardships and the dangers, but I remember that Naqua, in his prime, dared them successfully; and shall Tzihn fear to follow where he has led? Thy blessing and the prayers of our people will bear me up. Thy spirit and theirs will be with me to guide my feet, and the gods will protect their own! Doubt me not, my father."

Naqua shook his head and sighed.

"Words are like the wind," he said, "they go and come but no man knows where they rest. They are like shadows that climb the hills, ending in darkness. Thou canst not guess what I suffered and yet out of this land and far beyond the desert, a band of warriors and a troop of slaves gave me safe conduct and provisions. Thou wilt go naked and alone and hunted like a dog! I wish not to place this task upon thee to thine own undoing. The contemplation of thy death has shown me how much I love thee, and for this reason, I ask thee to weigh well what is before thee. Nor shouldst thou forget that which is with thee now, but will remain behind if thou goest!"

"What meanst thou, father?"

"Canst thou leave what thou lovest so easily? O Tzihn, I have marked how the lady Zaca clings to thee like a vine, and my hearts bleeds for thee. The sacrifice that I make is that of a dry log, fit only for the fire; but thou art a young tree, full of sap and vigor, and to thee love is more than life. When I spoke to thee before and urged thee on, I had no thought of this. I saw nothing but the glory of our sacrifice and heard naught but the pitiful cry of our people. I heard not the moans of two riven hearts!

"O Tzihn, since then, light has come to me. I have spoken with the spirit of Tzebu and he has shown me the Great God. I know that our people seek a vain thing. They are in the hands of a mighty power that can save or destroy, and we waste our energies in striving too much after external aid. Man must save himself from within and not wait for the stars to fall. Save thyself while thou canst and return not to share the curse of Coyoa which is upon them for their sins. Naqua absolves thee from thy vow!"

The old man covered his face with his hands and his whole frame shook with emotion.

Tzihn's impulse was to fall upon his knees and bless him, but when he moved, a pair of soft arms encircled his neck and held him still.

His upturned eyes met those of Zaca blazing with lovelight, and though she spoke not, he understood what she would say, and his mind followed hers!

He rose to his feet, and in a voice that sounded like that of her he loved, said:

"O Naqua, thy words are the shadows of clouds that hide the face of the sun! Shall I return to Coyoa and tell the sages and people that thy resolution has failed for the second time?"

The old man grew cold at his words, but he spoke calmly as one who has resolved to suffer all and die.

"Thou shalt tell them, Tzihn, to turn to the Great God who alone has power to save them, and that the Skystone is a curse!"

"I know not the Great God thou speakest of, except it be Azzu, and he is nailed to the sky and powerless. I know that we were sent hither for a certain purpose and *that* we must accomplish!"

*   *   *   *   *   *   *   *

Naqua staggered back to the temple crushed and heartbroken. Tzihn's last words rang in his ears like a voice heard in a dream. There was no escape from the fulfillment of his vow except by death, and he prayed that this might come speedily. What if he should tell lord Huema of his predicament? No—it was one of those matters wherein counsel fails and only a higher power than man's can intervene. He must either deliver the Skystone to Tzihn or refuse outright to do so, unless death came to solve the problem!

When he entered the audience chamber, he found lord Huema pacing the floor like one distressed in mind.

He met Naqua and said: "Thou hast come in good time for I was about to send for thee!

"When the clouds gather in a circle and overcast the earth with ponderous mass, we prepare for the storm; but the cloud-burst comes from an open sky and gives no time for preparation!"

Naqua bowed and said to himself: "The cloudburst has fallen upon me!"

"That which I have feared these many years," continued lord Huema, "has fallen when least expected, and I am overwhelmed!"

"What meanst thou?"

"Sit thee down, O Naqua, for thou art feeble and shakest like a leaf, but let me walk, for my blood is stirring and I cannot be still. Since the overthrow of Ilome nothing has disturbed the peace of Mázacl, and I was led to hope that I should die before a change took place. When the Great Council met, complaints came only from Tzanahl and Coyal, and their grievances were at once adjusted.

"The first, which is the city of the Two Rivers, a day's journey from Yahvan, solicited the privilege of erecting a public granary for that district, so that the people would not be compelled to bring their surplus to the temple. While I believed it unwise in principle to permit the people to sever themselves from Yahvan, yet the matter was urged so strongly that I yielded, and forthwith sent builders to superintend the work.

"The grievance of the second, which lies to the west of the Stones of the Giants, was that the great canal took all the water when the river was low. I met this by giving orders to those in charge of the head-gates of the canal to let pass a certain flow of the water in the dry seasons. Nevertheless I knew that it was but a waste of water for before it reached their dam it would sink in the sand! These concessions, instead of pacifying them, bred new discontents, or rather gave them courage to make these known, and I sent the Lionhead to both places to learn the real measure of the trouble.

"Mark now how the small cloud has grown!

"Tzanahl having secured a granary, demands that the people be released from the obligation to come to Yahvan to celebrate the Feast of the Harvest, giving specious reasons therefor. Coyal, finding that the water sinks, as they well knew it would, asks that a new canal be constructed starting one-fourth of a day's journey above the present head-gates, ignoring the rights of intervening settlements whose priority is beyond question, and causing them to suffer for all that Coyal gains. It requires no great wisdom to perceive that these are mere pretexts and not the marrow of their contention, which lies deeper, as Lord Lionhead clearly intimates.   When I told thee that the people who came from the south mingled with our own, I spoke in a general way.   They really predominate in Tzanahl and Coyal and have given these places more of their own character than I thought.

"At the time they came among us we had small settlements along the river and at Ilome, and as there was much unoccupied land, they were permitted to settle in those localities.   In the course of years and owing to the lack of foresight on the part of the Chief Keepers of the Temple they concentrated at Ilome and brought on the catastrophe that culminated in their ruin.   To all appearance those that remained in their original localities lost their identity, but it is now apparent that they have preserved their traditions and after thirty years of peace and prosperity have forgotten the fate of Ilome, or remember it only as a grievance.

"There is no question that the outcasts have found means of corresponding with certain ambitious persons whose influence has been so secretly working that while the present outburst is sudden, it is in reality of long preparation.   It has developed a strength that has given them boldness and provoked them to make demands, reasonable enough to the ignorant, but which being denied, will furnish an apparently real motive for the rebellion they contemplate.

"The object of this rebellion is to form an independent government such as that which was obtained for

Ilome by similar methods. Whether they seek more than this I cannot say!"

"O Huema, we travel in circles!" observed Naqua.

"Thou sayest truly and if we seek to return always to the good, the faster we travel the better, but evil precedents should be reversed. It is better to be a wandering light that has no fixed habitation in the heavens than a falling star that wastes its glory in the air!"

"In my country, where the trees grow so thick and tall, with overhanging branches like a roof, the traveler is often unable to take his bearings and is lost. Then he travels in a circle, ever returning to the place whence he started. He will die of hunger if he knows not how to break the circle!"

"This is a treeless region and I can neither understand the circumstance nor guess the means of evading it."

"Yet it is simple. Sighting three trees in line, he stands near the middle one, sights back to the first and forward to another, thus on and on until the circle is broken and he reaches some favorable point."

"It is the method used by those who line the canals and fix the foundations of the walls. I thank thee for the suggestion. The circle can only be broken by pursuing a straight path. This I will do, and from the past line up the future! This incipient rebellion shall be crushed if there is power in Mázacl to do it! I know the old circle that our race has run. First, dissensions such as these, then the struggle for the Skystone and last of all the curse!

"If that cursed gem were cast into the great sea we might have peace and abide in the land of our fathers for ever!"   Then stopping suddenly before Naqua, he asked:

"Hast thou seen the lady Zaca of late?"

"I saw her but an hour ago."

"A suspicion awakes in my mind that she has correspondence with the outcasts. She is their natural head, and yet, being a woman, brought up among us, it seems unreasonable to suspect her fidelity. But at such a time as this we must see a foe in every bush. The outcasts have had comparatively free intercourse with the disaffected. We have been lax in this matter, but our diligence shall awaken. She and all others shall be closely watched! The air is full of strange sights and sounds, and we must have eyes and ears for all things!"

CHAPTER XXIV

THE favorite slave of Zaca spoke to her mistress secretly: "O lady, when the summer sun shone thou hadst but one shadow, and lo, in the dull winter days thou hast two!"

"What meanest thou, Huajua?" said Zaca sharply, for she thought the girl referred to Tzihn who was with her so much.

Huajua shook her head, answering the thought of her mistress.

"The second shadow is a servant of the temple who spies upon thee!"

Zaca started with alarm, for she dreamt not of this.

"How knowest thou?"

The girl put a finger under each eye and pulled them open so far that the whites looked like the shells of pigeon eggs.

"When the lady Zaca walks, I see him dodging along

the path like a *churrea,* or peering from behind the walls. .When she talks with the stranger, he stretches his neck like a *campamoche,* trying to hear what is said. Oh yes, I see him with these eyes!" and she pulled them open wider than before.

"How knowest thou that he is of the temple?"

"Under his cloak he wears a yellow girdle."

"How long has this been?"

"These two days."

"And why didst thou not tell me this before?"

The girl hung down her head and replied: "I had not yet guessed his purpose."_

"Thou art a good girl, and when thou art betrothed I will give thee a necklace of pink shells. Continue to be watchful!"

Since her visit to Tote's protege, Zaca had thought much of the strange child who talked with the birds, and she resolved to visit her again. Tote had gone to Coyal with a message to Lionhead and was not expected back until the morrow, but he had charged Chácama to admit Zaca if she came.

Wrapping herself up warmly, for the afternoon was cool, she went forth with the girl, bidding her watch if they were followed by the man she had spoken of.

When the houses were scattered Huajua drew near her mistress and said: "If thou lookest to thy left thou wilt see his shadow fall beyond the wall of the house with a thatched roof!"

Zaca looked and saw beyond the shadow of the house, the shadow of a man.

"It is well!" she said.

When they reached the dwelling of Chácama, Zaca bade the girl remain outside until she returned.

She found the old woman lying upon a mat in the outer chamber near a smoldering fire, groaning with agony, for the pains in her bones gave her no peace.

"How does the little one?" Zaca enquired.

Chácama shook her head and sighed.

"The birds are sad to-day and will not eat for she has not been near them. Their feathers droop as when it rains and they make doleful noises. All night a dry racking cough gave her no rest, and to-day she is too weak to rise. O lady, I see shadows moving about the house where none should be, and I fear that the gods have sent for her. I crawled to the side of the couch just before you entered, to be sure that she was alive. She heard me come and said, 'Poor Chácama, rest thee, for I am well!' Ah, my soul—she is of the gods, and we cannot keep her!"

A twinge of pain set the old woman groaning again, and Zaca passed to the inner chamber.

The child lay upon a couch covered with warm furs, her head propped up with a pillow. Her hands were crossed before her and her eyes closed.

Zaca started for she thought she was dead, but while

she gazed, the child opened her eyes and smiled upon her.

"Thou art Zaca, the friend of Wunksh! I knew thou wert coming for I bade them send for thee. Come closer, for they are between us and I see them dimly."

"Who are they?" asked Zaca anxiously.

"I know not—and yet I know! They have faces like thine, only there are no shadows upon theirs—nothing but love! Their garments are like the feathers of birds; they move in the air like bright motes in the sunbeam, and the rustle of their garments makes music sweeter than the songs of birds! When I am alone they speak to me, telling me things that fill my soul with joy—things that I cannot repeat, for it is a language that my tongue knows not. When Wunksh holds me to his heart, he thinks he hears the music I speak of, and is happy!"

"O child, these are spirits of the world beyond that come to thee in dreams!"

"Not in dreams—for dreams come in our sleep, while these I see when I am awake! They are with me now —canst thou not see them? They smile at me, and hold out their arms! Place thy head against my chest and perchance thou wilt hear the music as Wunksh does!"

To humor her, Zaca did as she said, but heard only the breath rattle and rumble and the little heart struggle bravely but wearily. There came no music to her soul!

When she raised her head, the child's mind ran to other matters.

"Alas, the Wunksh will come too late! He hurries fast, but evil spirits hold him back. Where is Chácama? I remember—her limbs ache so that she cannot stand. It is an awful thing to grow old. Wilt thou grow old Zaca? Will thy face grow yellow and wrinkled, thine eyes become blear, thy hair grey and thy footsteps feeble?" A spasm of pain shook her frail form and she slipped down from the pillow. When it passed she gasped feebly and her eyes rolled as if they were sightless.

Zaca rested her cheek against that of the dying girl, and it was as if she pressed the soft leaves of a fragrant flower.

The rattling breath paused—a tremor shook the tender frame—the lips parted for an instant—then closed again—and the eyes opened and looked upon eternity!

*   *   *   *   *   *   *   *

When Zaca saw that she was dead she crept from the room, for a great dread fell upon her.

Chácama was sleeping upon the mat and muttering in her sleep. Without awakening her she left the house and found Huajua waiting her with impatience.

"O lady," she said, "the yellow girdled one is behind yonder bush!"

Zaca appeared to hear her not but walked on with nervous haste, and the girl said to herself, "Surely the old witch Chácama has prophesied evil to my mistress, for she looks as if she had touched the dead!"

*   *   *   *   *   *   *   *

When Chácama awoke it was nearly dark and a cold wind came under the mat. The short rest had relieved her pain somewhat and she was able to rise to her feet.

She hobbled to the fire, blew an ember into a blaze and lighted a lamp. With this she entered the inner chamber, upbraiding herself in a low tone for neglecting her charge so long. Her sight was weak, and when she looked at the countenance of the dead girl she muttered, "It is well—she sleeps!"

She drew up the robe that had fallen back from the little form, and setting the lamp in one corner upon the floor, hobbled back to replenish the fire.

"I will prepare a tea of herbs, so that she can take it when she awakes. Alas, if my master come not soon, he will come too late, for the air has the odor of death. Last night a star fell, which means that a spirit has been sent from above to save a soul from Mazzai, and what soul but hers is worth the saving!"

While she chatted to herself, the mat at the door was pushed aside and a man stealthily entered. He looked at the bent figure of the old woman by the fire for an instant and then entered the room where the dead child was. He bent over the couch and saw that life had fled. He raised the robe, looked at the twisted body and shook his head.

"This was the child of a slave mother who has avoided the law!"

At that instant Chácama entered and saw him!

Forgetting her lameness she sprang upon him like a young wolf. Pulling aside the cloak that he wore she exposed the yellow girdle at his waist, and a fury seized her.

With a wild cry of rage she clutched his throat with her long fingers and bit at him with her yellow teeth!

So sudden was her onslaught that the man was taken by surprise, but quickly recovering himself he exerted his strength and bore her back so that she fell heavily upon the floor, but without releasing her hold.

She continued to struggle fiercely, spitting curses and tearing at his face until he choked her into silence.

When she was still he rose breathless and sought to escape hurriedly by the door, but there stood the dark figure of a man with heaving shoulders and panting breath. His eyes blazed with the wrath of a demon and two long arms stretched towards the intruder pawing the air.

They seized him in an instant and seemed to squeeze out his breath, then he was lifted in the air and hurled against the wall!

There he lay like a log and Tote stood above him gloating over his death agony!

CHAPTER XXV.

Meek spirits bow until the storm goes by;
But fiercer ones hold up their arms and roar
Like the long waves against a rocky shore—
And spit their anger at the sky!

"THERE is a spy set upon me, and we must meet no more where we may be seen or heard!"

Tzihn smiled.

"Fear not, O Zaca, for the spy, like a thunder-cloud, has passed on, leaving our sky clearer than before."

"Thou hast heard something? Tell me it quickly for my nerves are unstrung and I see danger in every shadow."

"There is no danger, bright one, except in thy fears. Naqua came to me and told me of the spy. The lord Huema has been much disturbed of late with these troubles at Coyal and Tzanahl and thought that the disaffected might seek to communicate with thee. Therefore he had a watch set upon thy goings and comings. Learning that we met as lovers meet, and talked as lovers talked, he judged that in the sunshine of our souls no thorns of hate could thrive!"

"He is a fool," interrupted Zaca, "for love and hate are the twin shadows of passion!"

"After some thought," continued Tzihn, "he spoke of the matter to Naqua. 'If these two,' he said, 'can be induced to mate it will be an excellent thing. Thy friend is bound to thee, and thou to me, and if, as it appears, the lady Zaca loves him, we can make them one that shall be joined to us beyond all doubt!' To this Naqua replied that while the result was one to be desired yet there was an insuperable obstacle. I was a Moreover,' he added, 'the lady Zaca is not subject to wed thee.

"The lord Huema quickly replied, 'The law was made for the welfare of the people, but special occasions arise when their interests are best served by its violation. Moreover,' he added, 'the lady Zaca is not a subject to the law of Mázacl except so far as her own will goes.' "

"He is a shrewd reasoner," observed Zaca, "and like a lizard wears the color of what he lies upon. I shall store up this argument for my own use for it takes my fancy! What didst thou reply to Naqua?"

"I answered not at once, deliberating what I should say. Naqua urged me strongly to approve the scheme. He painted so truly the happiness of a life passed with thee that the sweetness of it made my heart heavy with longing; then against this he set the anguish of separation and the pangs of never-dying yet hopeless love that drags through the slow moving years like a wounded serpent. 'Here,' he said, 'are life and love, and there is death; for even if thou livest, thy heart will be dead

and when the heart dieth, life is like an empty gourd!'—
When he finished I begged for time to consider the matter."

"That was wise, for while we wait, much may come
to pass, and, at least, we shall go unwatched. Sooner
or later Naqua shall have his answer and it will be,
Nay! Zaca is not a slave to be bestowed even where she
would bestow herself, and my people would like it not
if they knew. Lord Huema understands them well,
and knows that if I, their natural head, am withdrawn,
they will contend among themselves for supremacy and
destroy one another. Truly Tacantla has sworn himself thy friend; but he cannot rule the minds of the
people. They will sometimes think for themselves, and
when they do, their leaders have to fall in with them
or be left behind.

"Thy deeds must commend thee to them so that thou
art beholden to no other man. If thou bringest the
Skystone to them, thou canst ask of them what thou
wilt—even Zaca! Shall lord Huema, the slayer of my
father; who has exiled my kinsfolks and ruined my inheritance—give me a husband? When I was a child,
he would pat me on the cheek and pity me—and therefore I hate him and all the cropped heads!"

*   *   *   *   *   *   *   *

Tote crouched by the door of Zaca's chamber like a
great bear. His hair stood up in bristling locks, his
eyes were yellow, and he snarled at his own shadow.

When Zaca came from Tzihn and stopped before him, he merely raised his head and stared at her.

"What ails thee?" she asked.

"I lie in the shadow of death! She is dead and Chácama is dead! The yellow lizard that poisoned them is in hell!"

Zaca trembled and turned pale.

In a low, muttering tone he told her how the spy from the temple had entered the house while Chácama slept and strangled her and the child.

His eyes blazed like balls of yellow fire; his long arms clawed at the air as if he were strangling men, and he panted like a tired dog.

"May the curse of Mazzai," he said, "hang over the land like a great cloud and shower evils upon it; may the false priests rot in their holes like stifled rats, and their harvests never ripen! I am Tote the Avenger and my throat is dry with cursing!"

Zaca listened to his raving in silence for her mind was working. She knew that the child had died a natural death and that the spy was innocent of all but Chácama's ending. The fragile life had gone out while she looked, like a spark of fire extinguished in the air. Was it not better to let him remain ignorant of the truth? His hate strengthened her cause. The gods, not she, had brought this matter about as she wished. If she had not gone to see the child, the child would still have died. Surely she was not to blame because

the gods had turned the visit so much to her advantage!
Chácama had been murdered ruthlessly, and this crime
ought to be avenged and to this extent Tote was justi-
fied in his anger. With this reasoning her personal fear
was dispelled and her contrition melted like frost in
the sunshine.

"I had worn the bonds of Mázacl so long," continued
Tote, "that I ceased to regard them—but now they gall
my flesh and sink into my soul!"

"Then break them!"

"That I will—but in my own way—treachery for
treachery! As they entered my home, to rob me of that
which was dearer than life—so will I enter theirs—
and they shall not know it till the roof falls and crushes
them!"

"Wilt thou not join with us now?"

"That I will—but in my own way, as I have said. I
shall work for thee O Zaca for evil or good, but I bind
myself to none!"

His words filled her with joy; she stooped and put
her hands upon his shoulders and breathed upon his
face—"My warrior and my cousin!" she said.

Then came a thought of Lionhead and Tote's love
for him.

"Dost thou number Lionhead with thine enemies?"

He turned his face to the wall and she saw his shoulders heave with the strength of his emotion. When he

turned again his lips were weeping blood for his teeth
had punctured them when he struggled with himself.

"There is nothing but hate in my heart for they have
destroyed the fountain of love. Let Lionhead beware
the Avenger, for hate is blind!"

CHAPTER XXVI

"The brown fox met a rabbit one day—
Oh, mother, what seekest thou?
Little Long-ears has gone astray—
I cannot find her! Help me I pray,
Help me to find little Long-ears!
And the dwarf-owl moaned,
Too-whoo! Too-whoo! Too-whoo!
From the top of a *saguara*.

The rabbit went to the fox's lair—
Oh, mother, what seekest thou?
Her little Long-ears was lying there—
Its fur was scattered, its bones were bare—
The brown fox had eaten Long-ears!
And the dwarf-owl moaned,
Ugh! Ugh! Ugh!—"

Tote sat upon the outer edge of the temple moat towards the west and hummed the song of the Fox and the Rabbit, keeping time with his feet, but when he came to the last refrain, instead of imitating the note of the owl, he laughed until his body shook.

"Why art thou so merry?"

The voice of the speaker came from behind him and he stopped suddenly and turned. The lord Huema, with Naqua and several attendants, stood there with wonder on their faces for none had heard him laugh before.

"

"O lord Huema," he said, "I sang the song of the Fox and the Mother Rabbit that the children sing. The rabbit was a fool to trust the fox and therefore I laughed."

"It is a poor song, but the moral is rich. We should· neither carry our misfortunes to our enemy nor ask of him a service!"

"Rabbits live in holes and are fools!" said Tote sententiously.

"I am glad I met thee," continued lord Huema, changing the subject, "for I have sent a messenger to seek thee."

"I am at thy service, O Huema!"

"Thou shalt bear a message to Coyal, to the Lionhead, with all speed. I have it with me, expecting the messenger to find thee speedily, so that nothing need delay thee but thine own preparation. This is the tablet thou shalt give him. It is of great importance, and I chose thee to bear it, because thou art prompt and faithful."

Tote took the tablet from him, and after holding it against his forehead, placed it in the pouch at his girdle.

When he was gone some twenty paces the lord Huema recalled him and said:

"The lord Naqua has urged me to give the stranger Tzihn license to go with thee if thou wilt have his company."

"It shall be as thou sayest."

As Huema turned away, Naqua whispered into Tote's ear: "If a certain matter referring to the lady Zaca be discussed between you, I pray thee urge him to abide by my counsel. If he mention it not, my words are unspoken!"

Wondering what the certain matter might be, Tote nodded his head and left.

When he was gone, Huema turned to Naqua and said: "I thank thee for thy suggestion, for we can depend entirely upon thy friend's integrity. While I doubt not the loyalty of Tote, for it has been well tried, yet in these troublous times he only is well armed who is doubly armed. So far he has been a faithful servant, ready to follow or lead, and may he stay so!"

"He is a strange fellow," observed Naqua, "hard to understand in his moods, but he appears to be well meaning."

"That he is! Brooding over his shape, which has set him apart from other men, gives him those moody fits. He makes few friendships, and his interest in life hangs upon his affections. For those he loves, and for their cause, there is no peril too great for him to undertake; but when there is no love he has neither sense nor motion!"

"I remember," said Naqua, "that when we were overwhelmed by the Tankmen as we came to Mázacl, he would not aid us till the last, and I wondered then if he had human feeling."

"He stirred not because your people had no interest for him; but at the end his soul was touched and then he saved you! If he should learn to hate he would be a foe to fear, for he has the cunning of the fox and the strength of the bison whose name he bestows upon himself. Only two have firmly won his affections—the lady Zaca, his cousin, and the Lionhead. If he serves others it is only because they will it. Didst thou not mark how cold he was to me? He loves me not, and yet, for the sake of Lionhead, he will make himself my slave!"

"The human mind is like the restless clouds, that wear all shapes and colors, but behind them lies the blue of heaven, wherein do dwell the sun and moon and countless starry gems!"

*   *   *   *   *   *   *   *

Tote found Tzihn sitting by the door of his room stringing a bow that he had fashioned from the limb of a mountain ash.

When he saw Tote, he called to him. "Come see the twisted stag hair which I have strung to the bow, and thou wilt never after use one of sinews that loosen when the air is damp and break with over-tension when it is dry. These they use in the south where the changes are frequent and sudden, but apart from this they are in many respects superior to the others." Then he began to explain the virtues of the hair, but Tote stopped him and said: "Set thy bow aside and put on thy sandals for we travel together!" and he led him into the room and told him of the journey.

Tzihn was elated, for the inactive life he led was wearying him.

"First," he said, "I will tell Zaca that she may be in peace!"

"She is here!" and Zaca herself stepped out of the gloom of the chamber as if she came through the wall.

Both started at her sudden appearance, for they knew not how she had entered.

"Whither go ye in such haste?"

"I go," replied Tote, "to Coyal with a message from the chief crop-head of the temple to Lionhead, and permission has been given to Tzihn to accompany me!"

"What is the message?"

"That I know not, for it is on a tablet, and I cannot read."

"I know thou canst not; but I can. Give me the tablet and watch without the door both of you."

Tote reluctantly unfastened his pouch and handed it to her and went to the door with Tzihn who knelt down to fasten his sandals.

When they had left the room Zaca glided back into the shadow and came to her own room by the secret door:

Here she drew out the tablet and read the message as follows:

"*I have read thy message, and understand what thou*

sayest. Call together the leaders of the malcontents, and reason with them as I have commanded. If they hear not the voice of reason, leave them and return to Yahvan with thy warriors. I have need of thee, and them."

It was written hastily with pencil, and when she had studied it carefully she erased the last clauses and, closely imitating the scrawl of lord Huema, wrote in their stead:

"If they heed thee not, seize them and bring them to Yahvan with thy warriors.

"Tote is unfaithful. Watch him."

"If this bring not trouble upon them all," thought Zaca, "and dig not a deep pit between Tote and Lionhead, I am a false prophet. When the gods send opportunities we must show that we are wise, or abide with the fortune of fools!"

She replaced the tablet and stole back so stealthily that they knew not that she had left the room.

She called to Tote and said: "Take back thy pouch and see that the tablet is safely in it, or it may befall thee to lose it as Tzihn did."

"I lose nothing," replied Tote sullenly, "but what I wish to lose," and Tzihn hung down his head.

Zaca understood then that he intended that the message should not reach Lionhead, but this suited not her plan; thereupon she said, "This thou shalt not lose, O cousin, for I have sworn that it shall reach him to whom it is sent!"

"If thou sayest—"

"That I do! As thou valuest my favor, see that in this thou failest not—for it is better for thee and me that he read it!"

CHAPTER XXVII

"O LADY, the lord Tzihn is returning!" whispered Huajua entering suddenly. Zaca sat in her room combing her long tresses with a comb of tortoise shell, and her eyes shone through the mesh of hair like distant night-fires through forest trees.

"So soon!" she said and smiled. "It was but yesterday that he left."

"It is he," replied the girl, "for he hath come! He spoke to me and bade me take thee his greeting!"

"Thou hast a bad habit of winding in thy speech, Huajua. Like the venomous viper of the desert, thou goest back upon the path to advance along it!"

"O mistress, I meant no ill!"

"I know it—but those who serve should waste no words! Go now and lead him into the court and tell him to await me by the elder tree. Afterwards stand without and see that none comes upon us suddenly."

With her hair hanging down her back like the rippling waves of the night-sea, when the moon first dims the stars, she stood before him.

The ravishment of her beauty so overwhelmed him that he sank at her feet and kissed the hem of her robe.

Her eyes shone with the triumph that fills the soul of woman when she is worshipped, and she looked down upon him tenderly.

"Rise, O Tzihn!" she whispered.

And as he rose her hair fell around him like a veil.

*   *   *   *   *   *   *   *

"What brings thee back so soon, Tzihn—and Tote, where is he?"

"He came with me to the canal towards the west, and his face grew black and he bade me go on alone."

"He went to the grave of the little one!" thought Zaca as she stifled a sigh. Then she asked, "What has befallen that you return so quickly?"

"When we reached Coyal, Tote sought the lord Lionhead and what passed between them thou mayst learn from him, for he told me not. Something it was that filled his soul with grief, for he has scarcely opened his lips since.

"While he delivered his message, I wandered around, viewing the city. Every man sat by his own house and as I passed they gazed upon me curiously; some with lowering brows and others with mocking smiles.

"I was returning to seek Tote when I came upon a group of men behind a high wall built for the ball game, but the balls lay idle upon the ground and none looked at them.

"There came one to them hurriedly as I passed and made a secret sign which was made known to me by the lord Tacantla when I was in the hills.

"They all looked at me, whereat I made the same sign, and wonder fell upon them. He that had just come, approached me and repeated the sign with deliberation, and I answered it as I had been taught.

" 'Thou art the stranger from the south,' he said, 'and thy name is Tzihn!'

"I answered in the affirmative.

" 'Thou returnest to Yahvan?'

"I replied that I did.

" 'Thou wilt see the lady Zaca there,' he said, 'and tell her this from those that watch and wait in the hills and by the rivers: the harvest ripens fast and there will be many in the fields to gather it. Our women weave corn husks into spheres, and when the new moon hangs like a child upon the breast of its mother, the fire balls* will ascend like eagles of flame from the sum-

---

*During the Indian troubles in Arizona it was a common remark that "the soldiers never found the Indians till the Indians found them," and the truth of this was sustained by the facts. Not all of the critics, however, knew that this was the result of the perfect system of signaling used by the Indians, by means of which they were able to telegraph information from Mojave to the Rio Grande. Every mountain peak was a sentinel post, each prepared with bundles of hay arranged in such a manner that when one end of a bundle was lighted the smoke bore it up in the air like a balloon. The code was based upon a numerical system, and the signals were understood and repeated from peak to peak and the movements of the troops faithfully reported.

mits of the hills. Let her count the stars so that she may see them when they fly upward into the night. Let her be ready, for though words may flow in council like a spring flood, this thing shall not fail!"

"I promised to tell thee and passed on. Then I met Tote and he bade me prepare to return at once to Yahvan."

"How looked he?"

"Like one who is crushed at heart! As a mother looks when Death robs her of her first-born. As I should look if I were to lose thee!"

"How did he bear himself upon the way?"

"At the base of the hill Huetzl which in old times did turn the river from its ancient bed, we rested for a moment, and watched the smoke of the evening fires rise from Coyal against the red rocks of the giants. While we sat a large tarantula came out to catch the failing sun.

"I raised a stone to crush it, but Tote caught my hand and bade me kill it not for it had done me no harm, and might have a soul!

"'Look,' he said, 'at its long, hairy limbs, its swelling back and bristling beak! It will sit there in the sun like a lizard drinking the air, as harmless as a fly. If enraged, it will spring at thee like a wild cat and bite and bite until its rank poison fills thy blood! 'Tis said that the young feed like the scorpions upon their mother's vitals, and fatten in her shell. If it be so, she is well served for generating monsters. If flies were as venomous as this beast, they would soon purge the earth of men!'

"By this I knew that his wound was deep and rankled him, and asked him no questions."

"Thou didst well, for in his bitter moods they anger him. But see, he comes! Leave us alone and he will tell me all."

Tote came slowly, walking like a crab, taking no notice of Tzihn as he passed out. He threw himself upon the ground near Zaca, without heeding her, and hid his face in his arms like a stubborn child.

She bent over him, so that her hair mingled with his own, and placed her hand upon his shoulder, but he moved not.

"O cousin," she cried beseechingly, "thou canst not hate Zaca who has loved thee since thou wast a child! When pain or sorrow stung thee, who but I gave thee sympathy? Turn thy face towards me and unburden thyself as in the days gone by. Thy grief is my grief—thy hate my hate! The heaviness of waiting and the gloom of death are upon me as upon thee; but the time draws near when the waiting will end and the gloom be dispelled like the shades of night before the sunrise!"

He turned his grey face towards her and muttered, "For me there is neither life nor death, neither night nor sunrise! I am like the river mud in the sun—I lie and crack until the water comes again and when it fails I dry and crack again. I have no life!"

"This is the folly of a dreamer. Thou canst not live in the world and have no life! Tell me what the Lionhead has done to thee?"

He sprang to a sitting posture as if he had been pricked with a needle; his hands clenched and his eyes flamed, "Curse him," he said, "he has turned his back to me as if I was a slave!"

Zaca stepped back and laughed in his face.

"I see thy life returns to thee!"

"I deserve to be mocked, for I have been a fool! I thought he loved me—and when he spurned me from him, as he would a yellow toad, my tongue clove to my mouth and my blood boiled. 'Go back to Yahvan,' he said, 'the eggs here are already addled and thou canst not hatch them!'"

"What meant he by that?"

"I know not, neither do I care!"

"Something there must have been in the message thou tookest, that turned his mind, and yet when I read it, I saw nothing of moment!"

"There is no merit in hating an enemy," said Tote returning to his former position, "and my rage has come back upon itself and wearied me. I shall lie like a serpent in the grass, and stir not until someone treads upon me."

"Wilt thou sleep while thy brethren battle for their rights?"

"They fight for what they love, or think they love. I love nothing—not even myself. I will go to the hills and live with my brethren, the bears and wolves. I like them better than men for they profess no friendship and tell no lies!"

He rose to his feet and began to move away like one dreaming, but Zaca stood in his path and made him pause.

"*She* has come to me in a dream!"

His eyes opened wide, and his breath came quickly.

"Why comes she to thee and not to me? I, that loved her more than my soul! When she was alive, her sweet face was ever before me, her voice in my ears, and my soul was like a field of young corn! Upon the plain, among the craggy hills; when the sun shone and at night, she was with me. Now I see her not, hear not her voice and my dreams are like the visions of a fool. I have sought her everywhere—even at her grave —and find her not. If I could see her, my soul would live again."

"I tell thee I have seen her!"

"Yet she loved me more than any living thing! How looked she?"

"Her face was radiant with the spirit-glow, but her eyes were heavy like a misty morn when the fields are damp—perhaps she grieved for thee!"

"Spoke she?"

"With the bird-like voice of life but mellowed by her grief! 'Tote has lost his soul, and till he finds it, there is a gulf between us!'"

"What did she mean?"

"Thy moody fits; this sullen hate, which like a desert shower doth waste itself! While they rule, thou art less than a man, and the spirits hold no intercourse with brutes."

"Am I become a brute?"

"If thou art not yet thou wilt become one soon!"

"O, Zaca, show me the path that leads to her!"

"Bury thy personal griefs and charge thyself with greater matters. Thy hate is that of the crushed worm that writhes and writhes, but stings not. Thy curses are the whistling of the wind, and thy resolutions rubber balls thrown against a wall. Thy soul has left thee because it wearied of thy groans! Man lives not except through others and because thy sympathies are dead thou art the shadow of a man. Thy brethren call thee to aid them to regain their liberty. Liberty is of the gods—therefore thou art called of the gods also! Thou hast set thy little self against the gods and the gods have made thee what thou art. She whose memory thou lovest came to me because my soul is in me and she can find it, but where shall she look for thine? Oh, cousin, let thy heart beat for the struggles of men, and even through thy sins shalt thou recover thyself, for it is better to do evil than to do nothing earnestly. Sin brings repentance, as the clouds bring rain, and through remorse thy soul will come again. The gods will rather forgive the man, who for a good cause does wrong than him who sits like a yellow fungus on a rotting log, poisoning the air with curses! Seest thou not, that life is a round of duties, self-imposed or ordered by our fate, and step by step we must climb up, and move more swiftly when we hesitate!"

"Oh, if I thought—"

"Cease thinking, and like a child, be led. Thou hast followed the wind, and it has guided thee to a desert; now let Zaca lead thee along the path of duty!"

And he said, "I will!"

CHAPTER XXVIII

Some little wisdom and conceit of man,
A callous conscience and a mobile face;
The art to stir men's passions till they rage—
And still with dextrous hand direct the pace!
These are the gifts that make men great and raise
The envy of small minds, or win their praise!

THE spirit of the dawn rolled up the starry curtain of the night, and rosy morn, from hill to hill tripped lightly to the west, bearing the daylight to the skies beyond.

Then rose the sun behind the purple clouds in solemn grandeur, like a god, and when he looked upon them, they turned to ruddy flame, and melted in the air!

*　*　*　*　*　*　*　*

The sunlight streamed in between the teeth of Ketecla, lighting up the cavernous depths of his throat, and Cautpat of Coyal stood with his face to the light blinking like a cat in the sun.

·Before him sat the sages of Ilome, and behind him were grouped the warriors of the hills eagerly waiting for him to speak ill of their enemies.

"Hear the good Cautpat of Coyal!" said Tacantla, "and let your minds feed upon his words."

Cautpat spoke in a low measured tone like one that draws upon his memory.

"O sages and warriors! I am the voice of my people who are your kindred and your friends. Generations have passed since we dwelt together beyond the red mountains, and we are grown strange to each other. We have been like pools in the river in the dry season, when the fires burn in the mountains and the sky is like a white smoke. The dry places hold them apart and they grow shallower in the sun; but when the floods come they unite again and form a stream, before whose mighty current the great trees fall and the rocks are ground to sand!

"O brethren! the roar of the flood waters is in our ears; we feel its breath ruffling our breasts, and we are coming together to overwhelm the pride of Mázacl and crush her power! The pools rise and widen, and the banks that she has built between them shall dissolve like the morning mist!"

A murmur of approval echoed through the cavern and rumbled back into the maw of the giant.

"O sages and warriors!" he continued with more vigor, "if words fail me when I try to picture our wrongs, look upon my countenance, for my feelings will make it eloquent when my voice is mute. It is needless to tell how many generations we have endured the slights and impositions of Mázacl! Our long-suffering shows that we loved peace above all things and if we now seek to assert our manhood, it is because the peace they offer us is more disastrous than war can be. Endurance has become a crime against ourselves and posterity, and self-assertion the noblest virtue! The heartless priests who fatten and grow lazy from our toil—who pretend to govern by the will of the people and hear no voices but their own—have presumed too far! They have pressed us to a point where we must decide whether we shall become slaves or strive to be freemen! The middle ground between is washed away and we choose to be freemen.

"Oh the treachery of the false priests! They are serpents that sit in their holes and hiss at the sun! They are spiders that dig pits in the ground and what living thing comes by, falls in and is devoured! They press out the souls of men with oppression and then call them brutes! They have made the land like a field of corn when the grain is garnered! It shall be cut down and burned, and the wild hogs shall gnaw at the roots!"

He paused for breath and Zochapan whispered to one that sat by him: "This man circles in the air like a hawk, before he strikes his prey!"

"He will come to the pith of the matter," was the answer, "if his breath holds out."

"But all these things," resumed the man of Coyal, "are known to you as to us, for you have urged them often. But we always replied, 'We are at peace!' and like bees made the honey whereon your enemies fattened.

"Our eyes are now open and we see clearly. We know that we were wrong—so wrong that the shame of it bears heavy upon us. We remember, though, that ye are our brethren; that the same blood runs in our veins and our fathers came to the land together. Now that the awakening has come, where will ye stand if we shall fall? It is for your interest as for ours that we should join our hands!"

"He has us there!" muttered Zochapan.

"We asked of Mázacl only a little water for our fields. Year after year, their farms have spread to the south and west until they touch the lower river. The great canal has been widened and extended to meet the needs of the new cultivations; and because of this the water has failed us earlier every season so that now our crops wither before the harvest if it rains not. When we complained the answer was, 'There are other lands!'—as if it were a small matter to break up our homes.

"Then we demanded what was just, and being moved to anger by their cold indifference, added new matter to our first complaint. Then the Lionhead came with his warriors under the pretence of investigating matters, but really, as we saw, to awe us into submission or bribe our leaders. This scheme failed, and the final outrage fell upon us! Two days ago, he called a council of the chief men and they went fearing no treachery. When they stated their grievances, he rebuked them with many words, and like a fox that befouls himself, grew angry with the rank odor of his own utterances. This provoked our people to show their teeth and raise their voices against the misdeeds of Má-zacl. They referred to their generations of faithful service and obedience, their self-abnegation and the eye of the god Tzebu which their forefathers brought into the land.

"But the wrath of Lionhead grew apace, and seeing that the council had become a wrangle of words, our people proposed to send a deputation to Yahvan to see the lord Huema himself and end the matter one way or the other. The Lionhead answered with a sneer, 'O men of Coyal ye shall all go!'—and called his warriors. They quickly closed around, being prepared. They beat back the people with their clubs, and that same night carried the chiefs like criminal slaves to Yahvan!

"The hearts of our people swelled with rage! Our women tore their hair; the old men raised their arms to heaven and called upon the gods; our young men dug up their spears, re-strung the bows of their fathers and talked of bloody war! O brethren, the time is ripe for action! Are the people of the hills ready? We know that their arms are strong, their spears sharp, their bows well strung and their feet anxious to tread the plains whereon their fathers walked! When they shout their war cry, their enemies tremble, the earth quakes and the air is filled with the spirits that wait for the souls of dying men! Our young men lack warlike experience and their valor is untried; but their souls are eager and they will follow where the warriors of Ilome lead.

"O sages and warriors stand with us!"

When Cautpat was seated, Zochapan spoke.

"O brethren, the evil days are falling upon Coyal as upon Ilome; but when Ilome cried to Coyal and Tzanahl, Save us! they answered, 'We are at peace! We have our crops to gather and new walls to build for our houses!' While the red blood of our fathers and brothers ran in the furrows of the fields they were sowing the seeds of the peace they loved. Now they reap a harvest of ball cactus, whose spears fly out upon them and pierce their soft skins and burrow into the flesh. This is the peace they sowed, while we fought for our rights! Shall we now run the risk of being destroyed again in order to save those who refused us help in the day of our need, or shall we answer them also, We are at peace."

He stopped and looked around, scanning the faces of the warriors, to note the effect of his speech. He saw that it was not well received and changed his tone.

"O brethren we are not so ungenerous! We have shown it in many ways and will show it now by giving them the aid they ask. But they owe us some reparation for what they have done. Shall we endure all, give all, and ask no return! I recalled the past, not to offend, but to prompt justice! We were the first to wage war against the oppressor and while these people have slept in their houses and eaten new corn, we have dwelt in holes like bears and eaten or fasted as the gods willed. We should therefore reap the first fruits of victory. This is fair, this is just! It is as if a man should ask for the harvest that he has sown!"

"Thou meanest," said Cautpat, "that the men of Ilome shall be first in the councils of the new people!"

"Thou hast said it."

"I am not authorized to grant so much!" replied Cautpat sullenly.

"O brethren," observed Tacantla frowning at Zochapan, "this is not a matter to be discussed now. It is wise to catch your hare before cooking it, for uncaught hares are hard to skin! When victory comes we shall not misuse it."

"Thy wisdom is of the gods!" exclaimed Zochapan and he walked back among the warriors.

"Thou shalt tell thy people," continued Tacantla addressing Cautpat, "that what they ask is given. Let your young men be ready, and such weapons as they lack we will supply. When the hour is come to strike, they shall know and while they wait, let them watch the hills!

"O sages and warriors, have I spoken your minds?"

A loud "Yes!" came from every throat and then each one turned to his neighbor.

Tacantla and Cautpat drew apart from the rest and conversed in low tones for a short time, after which the latter departed.

When Tacantla turned, Zochapan came from the midst of the warriors and said: "O Tacantla, since the passing of Cazoc, our warriors have no leader."

"Who has the claim of merit for the post?"

"They are like so many beans in a pod, none shall choose between them—but Cazoc was a cedar upon the hills—alas, that he is gone!"

"Bewail not his loss, for he was unworthy! Let them choose among themselves whom they will and if they fail to agree, I will even lead them myself. I have not quite forgotten the warlike arts of my youth and old as I am I can render good account of myself!"

The warriors conferred among themselves, Zochapan passing from one group to another, urging this in favor of one and that in favor of another, giving his own word for no man and seeing that none gained many voices. While this went on, Tacantla, whose thoughts were on other matters walked back into the throat of Ketecla, and reaching the head of the steps that led to the chamber of the pit, sat down and rested his head upon his hands.

There came to his ears from below the sound of heavy breathing as if someone was ascending the steps. He arose and peered down the tunnel but saw nothing **for** his eyes were old and the light dim.

"O good Tacantla, I seek thee!"

The voice came from the gloom and sounded like one that he had heard before.

"Who art thou that comest by the forbidden way?"

"I am Tote the Avenger with a message from the lady Zaca!"

In another instant he stood by his side panting from the exertion of ascending

He drew a tablet from his pouch and gave it to Tacantla.

"I know thee now! Stay thou here while I go to the light and read the message!"

When he returned to the council chamber the warriors were still seeking a leader, but he paid no heed to them.

"*O Tacantla,*" he read, "*he whom thou wilt see has joined himself to us and thou mayst command him as thyself. The other remains until he has accomplished his purpose. By the sign thou knowest.*"

"This is good news!" he muttered. "Tote is worth a dozen ordinary men and knows all the tricks of our adversaries. He can be trusted, or Zaca would not send him here. He has the cunning of the fox, the valor of a lion and the strength of a bison. What a leader he would make! These fools will settle nothing by their wrangling, and when men fail us, we are wise to choose a monster— Peace warriors!" he cried aloud.

The busy hum of voices ceased and they turned towards him.

"Have 'ye made your choice?"

Zochapan answered, "It is as I said; among so much excellence none can be made, for if one is chosen he protests that he is no better than his fellows. Thou thyself must lead them!"

Tacantla understood then the malice of Zochapan. He stood next to himself and would, perchance, take his place as chief of the council, if the gods called him to his fathers or the misfortunes of war pursued him.

"O Zochapan," he replied, "When I said that I would lead, I knew not that the gods would send a better one than I. As I went into the throat of Ketecla to pray to them, and while the petition was upon my lips, there came up out of the chamber of the pit, a man that has the cunning of the fox, the valor of the lion and the strength of the bison."

The warriors drew closer together and whispered among themselves, "Surely it is the spirit of Cazoc returned to earth!" but Zochapan suspected that Tzihn had been sent by Zaca, and asked: "What is this gift of the gods called—if he has a name?"

"For many years he has been called the Bison of Mázacl, but now that his heart is changed, he is named, Tote the Avenger!"

Every man looked at his neighbor and Zochapan threw up his hands angrily. "What," he exclaimed—"the monster, the horned toad, the renegade, the friend of Lionhead, the servant of the priests of Yahvan! who smote thee in the face and pulled thy beard, even where thou standest! He who turned his red hand against his kindred—who has boasted in our teeth that he is an enemy—who has sneered at the warriors thou wouldst have him lead, calling them women and dogs!"

"Even he! The lady Zaca commands it, and I commend it. True, he has been our enemy, but he is now our friend. As we feared his arm when raised against us, so shall we love it when its power is against our enemies. He is no renegade for he never knew our cause before, and therefore could not be a traitor to it. Now the gods have shown him the justice of it and he comes to fight in its defence. In this he has done nobly and deserves our admiration not our contumely. If his form lacks beauty it has strength and agility which are more useful. Beauty of form may please women, but it will not turn the point of a spear nor smite the enemy. Do not our warriors make themselves hideous for battle in order to strike terror into the hearts of their enemies?—and because nature has endowed him beyond our art, shall we refuse him? Accept what the gods have sent ye and cease contention!"

There was wrath in the eyes of Zochapan as he

turned to the warriors and cried, "O warriors, will ye follow the monster or the lord Tacantla?"

"We will follow Tacantla!" they answered. "We want no hunchback!"

Zochapan turned to Tacantla with a grim smile, saying: "Thou hast heard! They love thee too well to set thee aside for a hunchback. Let him go back to the gods that sent him!"

CHAPTER XXIX

"When the days of your friendship are longest,
    When your lips by love's kisses are pressed,
Death is near with his jav'lin uplifted,
    To thrust its keen point in your breast.

"For every pleasure is fleeting,
    All sweetness turns bitter or sour;
The good things of life are inconstant,
    And fade like the bright desert flower.

"When the promise of hope is the fairest,
    When the sun of your glory is high,
The storm-god hovers above you,
    To blot out the beautiful sky.

"All earthly glory is fleeting,
    And hope is as fragile as bright,
Its promise as vain as the sunset,
    That ends in the gloom of the night."

---

*"Oh that those living in friendship
    Bound close by the thread of their love,
    Could see the sharp sword of the death-god!
    For surely pleasure is fleeting,
    All sweetness must change in the future
    For the things of life are inconstant."

---

*From an Aztec poem by *Nezahualcoyotl*, King of Tezcuco.
Mine can hardly be called an adaptation—it is merely suggested
by some of the lines.

Zaca reclined upon a mat in her chamber, with a lamp by her side, and in her hand she held an engraved tablet wherefrom she read the song of Nezah the chief poet of the temple whose words were always as if he looked upon life through the smoke of urn-fires.

"The gods are wiser than men," she reflected as she laid the tablet aside, "for they make an end of all things, while man strives through a long life and ends nothing, not even himself."

She rested her head upon her hand and the sleep god touched her senses and her thoughts merged into dreams.

She dreamt that the sun came down upon the temple and consumed it; she stood by the moat and saw the great flames that licked the beams with fiery tongues, and wondered why she felt no heat. While she gazed, Tote appeared in the midst of the flames that circled about him like feathers in the wind; his eyes were full of peace as he stretched his arms towards her and cried, "O Zaca, in this fiery furnace, I have found my soul!"

*   *   *   *   *   *   *   *

She was awakened by a light touch upon the shoulder and saw Huajua, the slave girl, kneeling beside her.

"O mistress, the wick of the lamp sank into the grease and the light was so great that I feared you might be burnt—therefore I entered. See, I have changed the lamp for another."

"Where hast thou been?" asked Zaca dreamily.

"I went to deliver the featherwork which thou gavest me for the wife of Lionhead."

"Has the Lionhead returned?"

"He has come with his warriors, bringing certain men of Coyal to answer for great crimes. One of the warriors told me that they had tried to drink up all the water in the river; but this I cannot believe unless the river is dry."

"Hast seen the Lionhead?"

"Yes, mistress."

"How looked he?"

"As black as night! When he entered where I sat with his wife, he scarcely regarded us, but threw his girdle and jacket upon the floor and bade her prepare food. Then he went into another chamber. His wife called the slaves and went with them, leaving me alone, whereupon I returned."

"Dost thou love me, Huajua?"

"O mistress, thou knowest!"

"Then do this thing for me. Thou sayest he threw down his girdle—did his pouch hang to it?"

"Truly it did. It is made of beaver skin and I saw it glisten in the light."

"Canst thou fetch me that girdle or the pouch alone without being observed?"

"I believe I can."

"Behold this armlet of turquoise and topaz. It is

worth fifty measures of corn. It is thine, Huajua, if thou fetchest me the pouch!"

The girl's eyes danced as she gazed at the armlet and with a smothered cry of joy she skipped from the room to earn it.

Zaca thanked the gods for the thought that had come to her like an inspiration, and prayed earnestly that the opportunity would not pass unused. The Lionhead would not enter the temple so late, but in the morning he would see Huema and show him the altered tablet. What might follow she could only guess; but the possibilities were dangerous.

The girl returned and found her mistress pacing the room like one beside herself. She drew the pouch from beneath her robe and Zaca almost screamed when she saw it.

"Quick," she whispered to the girl, "stand by the door until I call thee!"

Her nerves steadied in an instant, and she set to work to complete what she had begun.

Carefully erasing what she had written before, she retraced the words of Huema with such skill that the tablet looked as if it had not been touched.

She recalled the girl and bade her return the pouch to its place so that none might know that it had been tampered with.

"The gods are bountiful! That tablet has become the fate of Mázacl. It has set Tote against Lionhead and provoked the people of Coyal to rebellion. If I do not err, it will raise a wall between Lionhead and Huema that will keep them apart until the work is done!"

* * * * * * * *

The lord Huema passed a sleepless night, and before the dawn broke he arose and replenished the fire that smoldered in a corner of the chamber, and stood over it rubbing his hands together.

As the blaze flickered on the wall and along the floor, he espied the recumbent figure of a youth.

"Youth," he said, "has few cares and such as it has are soon forgotten. He will sleep soundly if the roof falls, while I, to whom sleep is the most needed nourishment, wander through the night with the eyes of an owl. O Mizpah!" he called aloud, shaking the sleeper, "awake!"

The youth yawned and stretched himself; then turned upon his back and snored.

"Awake, I say!" and he shook him so violently that he sat upright and stared at his feet as if he wondered whose they were.

"Awake thee, lazy one!"

The well-known voice penetrated to his brain and his torpid senses awoke. He sprang to his feet and stammered an apology for his slothfulness.

"Perhaps it was envy of thy rest that made me awaken thee! But go now and ask the lord Naqua to come hither, if he be awake, and then see if the Lion-head is come."

In a little while Naqua entered, showing in many ways that he too had been keeping vigil with the owl.

"Peace to thee lord Huema!"

"And peace to thee, my friend! I have sent for thee to help me charm away the time which is heavy with me. Let us sit by the fire, and like young hunters, count the game we will kill—

"Thou knowest how matters go in the West! I fear that the people of Coyal and Tzanahl will be stubborn, relying upon the support of the Outcasts. These, in their turn, have some alliance with the nomadic savage tribes that haunt the eastern hills. If this affair progresses far enough, as it bids fair to do, they will endeavor to divert attention from Coyal and Tzanahl by marauding the outlying settlements; destroying the canals and doing what other mischief offers. To prevent this we could make a general call upon our people; but this is a step I am loth to take, nor could it be done without first calling a general council. This would consume time when prompt action is the gist of the matter. What wouldst thou advise?"

"O Huema, in time of sudden trouble much council is to be avoided, for there is weakness in numbers as well as strength. The many move slowly and strike hard, but the few are swift and find the enemy unprepared. A fever of the blood is past curing when it has once gained the mastery, but it can be abated at the beginning by the application of the right remedies."

"Thou echoest my own thought; therefore, I shall summon no council. The marrow of the matter lies in the Outcasts. Of late they have made no overt attempts upon our peace, upon which fact I built vain hopes. I see now that they merely nursed their wrath. The Lionhead warned me of this, but I preferred to think the best of them. I have now recalled him and will send him in all haste to attack them in their homes, destroying them before they can move. Their destruction will break up the conspiracy, for the people of Coyal and Tzanahl are unwarlike by themselves and we shall have time to take precautions against any future trouble."

"It is a well-conceived plan," observed Naqua, "and ought to succeed. But see, here comes the Lionhead."

The warrior came towards them with long strides and after giving them peace, addressed Huema.

"O Huema, I have done thy bidding, and may the gods prosper it! I have seized the chief men of Coyal and brought them like slaves to Yahvan; but it has grieved me to the heart to see that thou hast withdrawn thy confidence from me."

Huema placed his hand upon the folded arms of the speaker and looked enquiringly into his face.

"What dost thou mean? I gave thee no command to seize the men of Coyal and bring them here! I rather desired that they should be left in peace—charmed by thy words into security. To arouse their ire at this juncture is folly. If thou hast done this thing, the re-. proach is with thee, for I am guiltless!"

"O Huema," replied Lionhead haughtily, "I am not dreaming nor am I filled with strong wine of corn! I have said that I did thy bidding according to thy message wherein thou didst further say that the messenger, whom I loved, was unworthy."

"By the Great God!" cried Huema stepping back, "I sent thee no such message, as Naqua will bear witness for he saw it."

"Thou thyself didst teach me to read and canst vouch for my proficiency. What was set down upon the tablet was as plain as the sun at midday. Yet so much I doubted the evidence of mine eyes that I read it over and over until there was no room for doubt. While my judgment revolted at the command, I could do no less than obey it."

"I repeat, that I sent thee no such message!"

Lionhead smiled coldly and answered: "I have it still and if thy command is not as I have said, I am a liar and no longer worthy to lead the warriors of Má- zacl!"

"Produce the tablet, and my life upon the truth of my words, unless it has been altered."

"That is very improbable for it left not the hands of Tote, and he cannot write. But here it is and thou shalt see."

Huema took the tablet, and when he had read it he passed it to Naqua who read it also; then both looked strangely at Lionhead.

"What hast thou done!" exclaimed Huema. "The tablet is as it left my hands—nor could it be otherwise!"

"By the gods, thou playest with me! Give it me that I may read it to thee, for perchance the rheum of age beclouds thy vision!"

He snatched it out of the hand of Naqua and his eyes blazed with fury as he read:

"I have read thy message and understand what thou sayest. Call together the leaders of the malcontents and reason with them as I have commanded. If they hear not the voice of reason, leave them and return to Yahvan with thy warriors. I have need of thee and them."

The tablet fell from his nerveless grasp and was shattered upon the floor!

CHAPTER XXX

"OH, TZIHN, the gods are upon our side, for surely that which has happened is from them! There is coldness between lord Huema and the Lionhead who has shut himself up in his chamber vowing that he will lead the warriors of Mázacl no more. But the warriors swear that no other shall lead them; and the affairs of Mázacl are like rubber balls that fly between the players and the wall!"

"Naqua has told me all!" replied Tzihn. "The Lionhead read not well the message sent by Tote and has wrought confusion. The lord Huema is willing enough to forgive the error, but Lionhead frets and fumes and is deaf to all reasoning. His pride is wounded to the quick and like a bruised serpent he bites himself and hisses at the air!"

"What is evil for Mázacl is good for us! Thou shalt give Naqua his answer to-day, for when the enemy is weak every blow counts. When thou hast done this we will know what is before us and act accordingly. See, there he comes, as if our thoughts had called him! His head is bent forward as if his heart trembled! Give me thy hand—thus!—now turn thy head away and look distressed—When I drop thy hand let simulated grief moisten thine eyes! When he speaks, let heavy wrinkles line thy forehead, like thunderclouds above the rain!"

Naqua raised his head as she moved slowly away and saw her.

"O Tzihn, peace!"

"There is no peace with me, father, for between my duty and my heart's desire, my soul is rent!"

"Let thy duty go hand in hand with thy desire, and then thy soul is whole."

"Would to the gods, it could be so! But as Azzu is pinioned in the sky for the sins of men so is Tzihn to his duty by the vow we made together. I wring my heart for my people when I turn my face towards Coyoa!"

The countenance of Naqua fell, and he looked sadly at Tzihn.

"My son, the time is unpropitious for thy wish. Who can tell what the gods will bring in a day."

"Thou biddest me wait?"

"There is no remedy but patience."

"I am weary of waiting!" said Tzihn doggedly. "Thou treatest me as if I were a child. Either thou wilt give me the Skystone or thou wilt not. Answer me directly so that I may know what is before me, and act accordingly."

Then Naqua saw guile in the heart of Tzihn, and his sadness changed to anger.

"I say, my son, that thou shalt wait. To gratify thy whim I cannot ruin those who have honored me beyond their own. The loss of the Skystone at this time would ruin Mázacl. If thou choosest to wait, it is well; if not —the matter is with thee!" and he turned and left him.

Tzihn immediately sought Zaca, and told her what had passed.

"I warned thee of this," she said, "and yet we must obtain it, for without it, thou wilt have no merit with my people."

She was silent for a moment, and then continued: "Thou knowest of the tunnel that leads from the pyramid to the temple! The entrance is easy, and once within the building it will be strange if thou findest not some means of reaching the stone. Thou hast the signet of Huema still and it may aid thee in thy quest. When I studied in the temple I knew the interior well, except only the upper chambers which we were not permitted to enter. This is the third story from the court and I have heard that the Holy Chamber is reached through many winding passages. Where the tunnel from the pyramid ends within the temple I know not, but once within, the way will be easy to find. Thou hast but to ascend as speedily as possible. At the worst thou canst seize one of the priests and make him guide thee, and when thou hast the stone it will be upon thine own

head if he betray thee. The confusion that now reigns
in the temple, as without, will aid thee—and remember, the gods are with us!"

*   *   *   *   *   *   *   *

Tzihn provided himself with a torch of twisted fibre
dipped in grease, a lighted punk stick and a short javelin. Under cover of darkness he sought the entrance to
the tunnel and found his way stopped by a wooden door.
He thrust the javelin through one of the cracks and
discovered that a bar of wood crossed it on the inside.
In a few moments he worked this out of its fastenings
and the door swayed. He pushed it aside far enough to admit him and propped it up when he had entered so that
if he returned hastily a slight touch would open it. Then
he blew his punk stick into a blaze and lighted the
torch. The passage was an arm's length in width and
of the height of a man. The two sides came together
gradually at the top like a pointed arch. For about two
hundred paces it made no change, but at this distance
it descended slightly, the walls being buttressed with
stout posts and the roof supported by crossbeams and
lagging. This led him to suspect that he was passing
under the moat and his suspicion was confirmed when at
the end of a few paces the tunnel rose at a steep angle.

He stopped and extinguished the torch fearing that it
might betray him as he entered the temple.

The darkness was intense but he stumbled upward

until his hands no longer touched the walls of the tunnel and he knew that he was within the temple.

He listened intently for any evidence of the presence of men, but the silence, like the gloom was profound. Satisfied that he ran no risk, he relighted the torch and saw that he was in a narrow chamber about six arms' lengths in height with walls as smooth as glass, but no visible opening except that by which he had entered. He raised his torch above his head and saw a black hole in the roof against the wall, but there was no ladder by which to reach it. This, however, was a small matter, for he could easily scale the wall. Placing his torch upright in the soft ground which formed the floor, he made holes in the wall for his hands and feet, using his javelin for this purpose, and having passed his head through the hole and found all silent above as below, he returned for the torch, and reascended.

He found himself in a chamber similar to the one he had left, and using the same method of ascent as before, he reached the floor above, where he found the ladder used by the people of the temple. According to his calculations, and the information given by Zaca, he had one more story to scale before reaching the floor upon which the Holy Chamber was situated. From the room in which he stood a door led into another, but he reflected that, if he wandered aimlessly about the temple, he would waste much valuable time and run the risk of being discovered.

His observation of the temple from beyond the moat had shown him that the buildings rose in terraces to the center; if, therefore, he could reach the roof of one of these he could ascend to the next with safety and without being bewildered. This he resolved to do, and searched for an opening in the wall that would afford a means of egress. He found one in the adjacent chamber, but barely large enough for his body to pass through.

He extinguished the torch and with some difficulty gained the roof of the building below. From here he ascended easily to another, taking careful note of his surroundings. A new difficulty now presented itself.

While the buildings conformed generally to the terracing, the detail was so irregular that he was not certain which terrace he was on. Considering that it was an advantage to be above, rather than below the floor he sought, he ascended still higher, and finding a convenient opening, re-entered the building. He immediately discovered that this portion of the temple was inhabited, for his feet pressed a mat spread upon the floor, and the next minute he stumbled over the prostrate body of a man. The man sat up and smote him, saying, "Canst thou not be still even in thy sleep?"

Tzihn stirred not from where he lay, until the man fell back and grumbled until he snored. He crawled along cautiously until he came to a wall, which he followed to a doorway, through which he passed into another room. The difficulties of his task now presented themselves to his mind in all their bearings.

It was easy enough, as he saw, to enter the temple, but unacquainted as he was with its interior, he might wander about even in daylight, and fail to find the locality he sought. · While the signet of Huema might avail him in an extremity, it was no means to his end. Zaca had been too sanguine and had underestimated the task. The gods might or might not be with him, but it was better to realize the circumstances as he found them and retrace his steps before he became hopelessly involved in the labyrinth of chambers that appeared to have neither direction nor end.

He was about to turn back when he heard the sound of voices to the left, and with the faint hope of receiving encouragement to remain, he crawled in that direction. The voices became more distinct as he advanced and in a few moments he saw a light ahead of him. He reached the door of the room whence it proceeded, and looking in saw Huema and Naqua seated by a fire. Their conversation ceased that instant. Naqua rose and lighted a lamp and taking leave of his companion came towards the door. Tzihn drew back into the shadow and when Naqua passed, he followed him until he entered his own chamber.

Naqua placed the lamp upon a wooden bench, threw off his upper garment and sat upon the edge of his couch with his back towards the door. The shadow of Tzihn moved along the floor and climbed the wall before him. He raised his eyes and saw it and started to his feet in alarm. Turning he beheld Tzihn standing by the lamp with folded arms.

A mournful cry came from his lips and he beat his breast in anguish, but Tzihn held up his hands and said: "O Naqua I am Tzihn in life. The death-god has not yet called me. I am come to fetch that which thou wouldst not bring me!"

"How camest thou hither? If thou art discovered—"

"It matters not how I came, and if I am discovered and condemned—upon thy soul be it. Know, that I leave not alive until the Skystone is in my hands."

"Impossible! The priests watch by the altar to-night and to-morrow night urging the gods to protect the land. Unhappy youth, why hast thou come! Fly by the way thou camest before thou art seen!"

"If one should come, I will tell him that I am here by thy connivance, and destruction will fall upon us together. Thou shalt thus keep the oath that we swore in Coyoa, to die rather than fail!"

"Oh, Tzihn, thou dealest hardly with me, but since thou wilt have the cursed stone, let it be as thou sayest, and the Great God be merciful to thee. I will conceal thee in yonder chamber, which has no opening but through this, until the night after next, and bring thee food and drink. Then I will fetch thee the Skystone and thou shalt go forth and look upon my face no more!"

CHAPTER XXXI

Life is a labyrinth, through which we climb
From what we dimly know to what we guess;
We pass from light to gloom, from gloom to light—
Our hope, the yearning of our soul's distress.

THE Lionhead* remained in his chamber, lashing his soul. His pride had been grievously wounded, and he said to himself: "Either the gods changed the writing to work me evil, or I am become foolish! If the gods are against me, my service will curse the land; if I am a fool I am no longer fit to lead men. In either case it is wise for me to hide like a wounded fowl."

The lord Huema came and beseeched him, saying: "The need of thee is most urgent. The enemies of Mázacl are ready to fall upon us and rend us. When they learn that the Lionhead holds down his head like

---

*The reader will probably wonder why I make so little use of such a promising character. I reserve him for the following work. He really had nothing to do with the Skystone, which is the subject of this story, and therefore could not properly be introduced fully.

A little reflection will show that I am right. He is a mere ghost in this story, but will materialize in the next.

I have been strongly tempted to make him more prominent, but my better judgment prevailed. Too many leading characters would spoil the play.

264

a maiden that has been wronged, even the cowards among them will become brave. What man lives who has not made mistakes? By our mistakes we become wise. Nor is that which thou hast made beyond excusing. The symbols of that which thou didst read and what was written are as much alike as the leaves of a tree."

"O Huema, thou offerest me honey that has lost its sweetness! It was no mistake, as thou knowest. I did not guess the meaning for I knew too well its evil consequence. The signs looked to my eyes as large as the furrows of a field. They are before my eyes now—see!" He stooped down and drew them in the dirt of the floor with his finger. "These are what I read and their meaning is plain. Truly, the spirits of evil are leagued against me and whom the gods have forsaken should not be followed by men!"

"It is incomprehensible!"

"And Tote, whom I loved! I spurned him from me like a dog. So faithful was he that he hung upon my footsteps like my shadow, waiting for my thoughts that he might serve them!"

"The blow fell upon him so heavily that he has fled to some solitude; but he shall be found and brought hither to comfort thee."

"I would ask his forgiveness."

"When thy grief has wasted itself, thou wilt see thy duty more plainly."

"Perhaps!" sighed the Lionhead and turned his face away.

* * * * * * * *

With the morning light Zaca looked for Tzihn and found him not. The day passed and another night, and still he was absent.

"Something has befallen him," she thought, "He is either lost in the chambers of the temple or he has been discovered and condemned. If he come not to-night I will send word to Naqua."

To those who enquired for him, she said : "He is gone with Tote!" But these enquiries were few for confusion reigned in Yahvan and each man thought of the trouble nearest to him.

When the second night came and brought him not, she wrapped a cloak about her and went to walk by the amphitheater, for the desire was strong with her to see the place where he had last walked. There was no doubt in her mind as to his fate, and she had urged him to seek it! The moon had just fallen behind the hills leaving a white halo of light, and a few stars shone between the drifting clouds. She descended to the arena and reached the base of the pyramid. She sat down and threw off her cloak for a fever was in her blood and her temples throbbed tumultuously.

"Oh, Tzihn!" she sighed, "that I should have sent thee to death!"

She threw herself along the sloping side of the pyramid and moaned in anguish. From moaning she turned to cursing; calling down the anger of the gods upon those guilty of his death, and threatening them with her eternal enmity.

This seemed to relieve her and she sat up and looked at the stars and the hurrying clouds and down again at the sleeping earth.

She started to her feet as she saw in the dim light a human form come across the arena from the north towards the opposite side of the pyramid.

As it drew nearer she recognized Tote.

Her first impulse was to fly to him for aid and counsel, but something restrained her and she waited to see what he would do.

He ascended the pyramid and reaching the top disappeared. She was immediately possessed with an uncontrollable desire to follow him. She reasoned against it, but before she knew what she had done, she was in the tunnel treading in the footsteps of him that went before.

"I go to Tzihn!" she muttered. "Tote knows where he is!"

Tote had no torch as Tzihn had, but he was more familiar with the ground and went straight ahead. When he entered the first chamber he felt along the walls and discovered the niches made by his predecessor. If he wondered at them he gave no sign, but quickly ascended by their means to the chamber above,

Zaca guided by his heavy breathing followed so quickly after that when he reached the next floor her hands almost touched his feet.

They stood in the same room together, but he dreamt not that she was by, for she breathed as lightly as a bird.

He deliberated a few moments and then passed out of the chamber towards the east, Zaca following as before, not daring to speak now for fear that he would spring upon her before she could make herself known.

After he had gone a short distance, he stopped as if in doubt, and felt along the wall.

She heard his hands gliding over the cemented surface, making a soft noise like the hiss of a serpent, and stood back until she knew which way he would take. The darkness was so intense that it seemed to have substance and press upon her. She felt a strong desire to cry out, and stuffed the corner of her tunic in her mouth.

Tote uttered a low grunt of surprise and the wall opened.

An old man came forth holding a lamp in his hand and the light fell upon Zaca, but Tote crouched behind the door and saw her not.

The man raised his eyes and saw her stand swaying before him like a white spirit!

Terror possessed him and he sank speechless to his

knees, the lamp falling upon the floor and being extinguished.

Before he could move, Tote sprang upon him!

He quickly gagged him and bound him with his own girdle, so that he could not move.

Then he entered by the door, closing it after him; but Zaca followed no farther, for she had swooned.

*　　*　　*　　*　　*　　*　　*　　*

A fire burned in the room, and by the light it gave Tote saw a jar of water and a gourd cup. He quenched his thirst and surveyed the place. The chamber was small and ventilated by a narrow window high up in the wall. On the side opposite to that on which he had entered was a wooden door fastened with a crossbar. He removed the bar and opened the door.

A man sprang out of the darkness, overthrowing him, and rushing to the fire seized a burning brand and waved it above his head, the sparks falling about him like a shower of stars.

"I am the sun!" he cried. "The earth is accursed and I will consume it! Roll back the clouds and let me pass—the sun-god is free!"

He pushed open the outer door and fled. This passed so quickly that Tote had only time to note, as he struggled to his feet, that the man was of great age and his sole garment a coarse cloth about his loins. It was evident to him that the room from which the man came led nowhere, and as his escape might alarm the servants of the temple he decided to retrace his steps and take another direction. He found the lamp that had fallen from the hand of his captive and lighted it at the fire. As he came back with it he beheld the form of Zaca stretched upon the floor like a streak of moonlight.

He recognized her when he came near and could hardly credit the evidence of his senses. How came she there! Had the cursed priests laid their rough hands upon her? When he found that she was only unconscious, his heart gave a joyful bound, and he was about to raise her and bear her away when he remembered the man that lay behind him.

He bent over him and said: "I will remove the gag from thy mouth so that thou canst answer me, but if thou criest out, thou diest!" and to emphasize the threat he raised a short club above his head.

The man made a sign to indicate that he comprehended and Tote removed the gag, but held his fingers about his throat.

"Tell me the way to the Holy Chamber."

"I know it not."

"Thou liest!"

The man gasped for breath as the fingers pressed upon his throat, and shook his head. It was plain that he spoke the truth.

"Where lies the Council Chamber?"

"In the second chamber beyond thou wilt find a ladder raised against the wall. Ascend it, and then two chambers to the right will bring thee to that which thou seekest."

Tote knew now where he was, and asked only one other question.

"Who is he that calls himself the sun-god?"

"He is the Tzah, the chief of Ilome, who has been a maniac since the day he was brought to Yahvan."

Tote gasped for breath and looked at Zaca. Her father must have stepped over her as he fled!

"The gods are in this!" he exclaimed; and then turning to the man he helped him to rise and bore him into the chamber of the maniac and barred the door behind him.

Returning to Zaca he lifted her up tenderly and carried her against his shoulder like a child to the foot of the ladder which the man had mentioned. Here he extinguished the lamp for it was dangerous to bear it further.

He ascended the ladder with his unconscious burden, and at the top came to a room lighted by the stars through a large opening in the wall.

He had been in it often when he came to the Council Chamber with Lionhead. It was curiously shaped, being formed out of three small rooms whose division walls had been partially removed. He laid Zaca down in a dark recess and rubbed her arms and hands vigorously and soon had the satisfaction of hearing her breath come regularly.

With a deep sigh she opened her eyes, and knew Tote by his shape.

"Thou art Tote?" she whispered.

"Ah, Zaca, it is I."

"Where am I?"

"In the temple. I found thee lying senseless and bore thee hither. Who brought thee to the temple? Tell me, Zaca, and his life shall pay for it!"

"Thou didst."

"I?"

"Yes. I saw thee enter the pyramid and followed thee to seek Tzihn who came by the same way two nights ago and came not forth again!"

"Why didst thou not speak to me?"

"At the first I could not, and afterwards I was afraid. Why art thou here?"

"I will answer thee hereafter. Peace now—for some one approaches! I will see who it is, and stir thou not from here until I return."

The reflection of a light grew upon the wall and Tote stole stealthily towards its source, keeping in the deepest shadow.

He saw the bent form of Naqua totter slowly along. A lamp swayed in his hand and he stopped frequently, looking nervously about him, as if he feared that he might be watched.

Tote followed him cautiously, forgetting Zaca in the excitement of his mind.

Naqua led the way through a labyrinth of chambers that appeared to circle about each other at different levels, and came at last to a sheet of red metal set in the wall like a door.

Here he halted, and placing the lamp upon the floor felt about the bottom of the door until he found a certain spot; this he pressed with considerable force and to Tote's amazement the door rose up into the wall leaving an opening through which a man could crawl.

Naqua entered, and Tote peeped in after him.

He saw a deep chamber whose sides and roof were wrapped in gloom. In the front center stood an altar covered with a mat of featherwork sparkling with gems, so that it looked like a bed of flowers sprinkled with rain-drops glistening in the sun.

Upon the top of the mat was a small casket, no larger than his two clenched hands—the casket wherein lay the Skystone, the genius of Mázacl!

Naqua knelt down before the altar and prayed aloud.

"Thou Unknown God who seest into the hearts of men as if they were clear water; thou knowest what thoughts move me to this deed, and in the life to come thou wilt hold me guiltless of intentional wrong. Through me may the curse depart from Mázacl and never reach Coyoa!"

He rose and seized the casket with trembling hand, and recovering the lamp that he had set down, moved towards the door.

Tote drew back quickly and waited.

When Naqua stood outside of the chamber, he set the lamp upon one side and the casket upon the other and grasping the bottom of the door with both hands, gave it a sudden pull.

It fell to the floor with a dull rumble like distant thunder.

He took up the lamp in one hand and with the other reached for the casket.

It was not where he had placed it!

He looked about upon the floor and felt with his hands, but found it not.

It had vanished completely!

But how?

The cold sweat beads stood upon his brow, the light danced before his eyes and his breath came fast, as the thought flashed upon him:

The Unknown God had answered his prayer and taken the Skystone from the world!*

---

*Perhaps it is not according to the accepted canons of good taste to leave the matter in this unsatisfactory state.

The reader will acknowledge that I have some good precedents and *history* arouses curiosity and never satisfies it.

CHAPTER XXXII

TZIHN had waited two whole days and nights, fearing for his life and worn with the conflict of passions.

Food and drink had been placed before him, but he hardly touched the first, it seemed to choke him.

His mind was perilously fitful, and he paced the floor of the vault like a caged lion, growing wilder at every turn.

In a few moments Naqua would return with the coveted Skystone, the possession of which would make him supreme among the people of Ilome and give him the right to claim Zaca!

But—supposing that he returned not, or came with a lie upon his lips!

His hands clenched and his eyes blazed with fury!

"If he deceives me, he shall die!"

A ray of light came under the mat that hung at the entrance.

"He comes!" he cried, and rushed out to meet him.

Naqua stood in the center of the chamber, his countenance as grey as his beard. His eyes were fixed as if he gazed inwardly upon his soul.

"O Naqua—bringest thou the Skystone?"

Naqua looked at him in a dazed way, and set down the lamp upon the floor.

"Hast thou the stone?"

The reply came wearily as if the speaker had done with the world:

"It is gone—I know not where! It was in my hands a moment; then vanished from my sight. The Great God has removed the curse from the world and my soul is at peace!"

An enraptured look fell upon his upturned face as he raised his hands above his grey head.

In that moment Tzihn lost his reason.

"Liar!" he cried, "Thy soul is on the edge of hell, while thou speakest. Thou hast hidden the stone!" and with a howl of rage, he sprang upon him and bore him to the floor.

The old man fell heavily and stirred not!

When Tzihn saw what he had done a revulsion of feeling took place and he knelt down beside him. He called him, Father; he kissed his hand and wept over it. He raised him in his arms so that his head leaned against his breast, calling upon the gods to bear witness to his love. No answer came to his caresses and the form of Naqua slipped from his arms like a dead thing!

When he realized what he had done in his ungoverned anger, he cursed himself and the mother that bore him.

He arose and drew back shuddering from the lifeless form of him he had loved—and killed. Not knowing what he did, he took up the lamp and passed through the door.

*   *   *   *   *   *   *   *

When Tote returned to the place where he had left Zaca he was astounded to find that she had disappeared.

He searched the adjoining rooms and even called her.

While he was despairing he saw the light of Tzihn's lamp and rushed towards it filled with desperate thoughts.

When he saw who it was, he called his name.

Tzihn heard him and asked: "Who calleth?"

"It is I—Tote! Tell me quickly, hast thou seen Zaca?"

The rush of events had so stunned Tzihn's senses that he did not even wonder how Tote came to be there, and why he should ask for Zaca.

"Zaca!" he repeated dreamily, as if the question puzzled him.

"Yes, Zaca! Art thou sleeping? She came with me into the temple to seek thee. I left her yonder a short time ago and now she is gone. Awake, Tzihn, if thou lovest her!"

Tzihn now comprehended, and the lamp shook so that the grease fell upon the floor.

Before he could reply, a wild cry rang through the temple, followed by the crackling sound of burning wood and the rush of hurrying feet.

"Put out the light or it will betray us!"

Tzihn obeyed.

"Now follow me! Something warns me that Zaca is in danger. The cries come from the roofs and we will seek them and learn what the alarm means."

Passing through several chambers, Tote led the way to the north side of the temple, and through an opening there they reached the roof where it overlooked the granaries and the court.

A cry of horror broke from them as they stood spellbound at what they saw.

Stacks of wood for the winter fires and heaps of corn husks and cobs had been piled in the court against the wall. These had become ignited and the fire had communicated to the granaries, so that the buildings upon that side were a mass of flame and smoke.

But this was the least of what they beheld!

Upon the roof of one of the buildings towards the east, stood an old man whose stature appeared gigantic and terrible between the forks of flame. Against his breast was pressed the white robed figure of a woman whose arms were stretched appealingly to heaven.

"Ye gods!" cried Tote, "It is Zaca in the arms of her father!"

"We will save her or die!" roared Tzihn seeing and

hearing only Zaca whose piteous cries, like a dying wail, rang in his ears.

"Save me! Save me!"

The Tzah waved his free arm in the air and shouted above the roar of the flame:

"I am the sun-god! This is my daughter, the moon! We go up to the skies in a chariot of fire and the earth shall be consumed for its sins!"

As he spoke the roof behind him heaved up from beneath by the heated air and swelling grain, burst with a thunder sound and the free flame leaped upward.

The maniac stepped upon a division wall and laughed at the furious flame.

"Save me!" shrieked Zaca.

A cry of horror rose from the people who stood upon the roofs and beyond the moat.

Then they saw two men creep along the roof towards the maniac and his victim. When they came six paces away, one, who had the shoulders and mane of a bison stopped the other and pointed to the roof between, swelling like a sea with jets of smoke spouting from the cracks.

Zaca saw them and cried: "Tzihn—Tote—save me!"

Tzihn prepared to spring across, but Tote pulled him back.

"If thou leavest the wall upon which we stand, she is lost! Stay thou here and I will cross and throw her into thine arms!"

He retreated a couple of paces and taking a great leap landed upon the wall by the side of Zaca and her father.

The people saw him wrest her from the maniac and heave her gently across the bursting roof into the waiting arms of Tzihn who bore her swiftly away to safety.

A yell of admiration rose in the air and all eyes turned to Tote.

The Tzah, angry at losing his prey, turned upon him like a demon, and Tote ran along the wall seeking a chance to spring back across the roof.

He bent his body for the leap when he was seized by the waist and pulled back.

Clouds of black smoke hid them for a few moments and a great report showed that the other roof had burst.

When the smoke changed to flame, the people saw two forms upon the wall with hair and clothes afire, groping like blind men, and both fell into the furnace and were seen no more of men.

END OF THE SKYSTONE

APPENDIX

As it was part of my theory that these people were the progenitors of the Aztecs I designed to give the characters Aztec name and titles, with such modifications as would be consistent with their antiquity. After reflection, however, I concluded that names that would be significant, were beyond the reach of the American reader; I have, therefore, deliberately invented names or cut down names in such a manner as to make them pronounceable.

The impossibilities of the language may be guessed from the following transcript of the Lord's prayer in the Nahua language:

Totatzine yuilhuicac timoyez-tica mayectenehualo inmotocatzin; mahualauh inmotlatocayotzin, machihualo intalticpac inmotlanequilitzin, inyuhchichihualo iuilhuicac; intotlaxcalmomoztlae totech monequi maaxcan xitechmomaquili; maxitechmetlapopohuili intotlatlacol, iniuh tiquintlapop olhuia intechtlatla calhuia; macamoxitechmomacahuili inicamo ipan tihuetzizque inteneyecoltiliztli tzanye xitechmomaquixtili inyhuicpa inamoqualli.

Nevertheless the language is sweet to the ear, and is said to be very expressive, abounding in tropes and metaphors.

I passed some time with the mountain tribes of central and southern Mexico, who probably speak some modification of the ancient language, and find them a fine people. To me their language sounded like music, and I judged from the translations made to me in Spanish that it was exceedingly metaphorical and full of illustrations from nature—such as I have used in this work.

It will be noticed that the language lacks the R and S.

THE GOLD OF OPHIR

BY

D. HOWARD GWINN

Cloth, $1.00

THIS is the promising production of a new Western writer, who depicts the stirring scenes of the mining camp in the palmy days of Leadville, and weaves a fascinating story of individual experience fraught with danger and adventure, culminating in a wild flight from Indians down the raging Colorado on a raft. The second part of the story is, if possible, still more breathlessly interesting, when the adventurers find a small Eden in a rock-walled cove of the Colorado, and later on a network of subterranean corridors and chambers containing astounding revelations of the " Lost Ten Tribes " and the history of their beautiful queen Corinthia, plotted against by envious rivals, who compass her downfall temporarily, but reap at last a just retribution.

For sale everywhere, or sent post-paid on receipt of price.

F. TENNYSON NEELY, Publisher,

96 Queen Street, London.   114 Fifth Avenue, New York.

SCHOOLED BY THE WORLD

BY

S. P. CHALFANT

&

Cloth, $1.00

&

THIS is a story woven from the realisms of life. Before reading many pages it becomes apparent to the reader that the author himself has been so schooled; that he has passed through many vicissitudes and adversities, mingling with all kinds and classes of people—for none other could write just such a book as this. It carries one through many different phases,—leading him even behind the scenes, so to speak,—and tells of human beings and existing realities of which much is known, yet which are so poorly understood. The author has told, in a very graphic and interesting way, how the noblest natures are often perverted by a selfish world, and makes of an honest though sensitive and high-strung youth a criminal trickster as well as a desperate outlaw. The book is written in a very thrilling and attractive style and can be read by all classes with both interest and profit.

THE SINS OF A WIDOW

BY

AMELIE L'OISEAU

Cloth, 25 Cents

THIS is a charming little story of social and moral conflict. The mental drawings in pen and ink have a touch of color that gives spice and yet pathos to the pages. It is a volume of snap-shots of society, toned with a solution of sense. Each grain of thought grows side by side with a bit of chaff. In fact, there is not any necessity to write at length of the book, as it speaks for itself. The charm lies not in its deep literary merit, but in the purely natural treatment.

THE SIGNOR

www.ingramcontent.com/pod-product-compliance
Lightning Source LLC
Chambersburg PA
CBHW020928120726
47905CB00008B/2429